HEY, DIDI DARLING

S. A. KENNEDY

 PUFFIN BOOKS

Puffin Books, Penguin Books Ltd, Harmondsworth, Middlesex, England
Viking Penguin Inc., 40 West 23rd Street, New York, New York 10010, U.S.A.
Penguin Books Australia Ltd, Ringwood, Victoria, Australia
Penguin Books Canada Limited, 2801 John Street, Markham, Ontario,
Canada L3R 1B4
Penguin Books (N.Z.) Ltd, 182–190 Wairau Road, Auckland 10, New Zealand

First published in the USA by Houghton Mifflin, 1983
Published in Puffin Books 1986

Typeset in 10/13 Linotron Sabon
by Rowland Phototypesetting Ltd,
Bury St Edmunds, Suffolk
Made and printed in Great Britain by
Cox and Wyman Ltd, Reading

1

It was Renee's idea, really. No it wasn't, it was mine, of course; but she inspired it.

The group was sitting around at my house in the rumpus room (my mother is the one who started calling it this; even though it's still the basement) after a really hot jam session. It was the kind where you absolutely *know* that you are sounding good. There we were, relaxing in the afterglow and enjoying our Cokes, when Renee had to break up the mood by starting in about our name.

'The Teenettes,' she sneered.

Renee cannot talk without sneering. For the tenth time, with incredible patience, I explained:

'It's *supposed* to be dumb. That's very hot now. It's called nostalgia.'

'Nostalgia! What do we have to be nostalgic about? We weren't even born in the fifties.'

Then Jan spoke up timidly but firmly, which is the way she does, and said, 'The thing is, Tammy, most of the kids at school don't read *Billboard* and *Rolling Stone* the way you do. I bet lots of them have never even heard of nostalgia.'

'They watch "Happy Days", don't they?' I said bitterly. I was hurt. I know Jan likes everybody, she can't help it. But she's supposed to like me the best. She's my best friend. And here she was, siding with old sneering Renee.

Did she think we should let Renee pick the name?

When we were reorganizing the Swanson Junior High girls' hockey team Renee said we should call ourselves the TV Dinners. That's how good she is at picking names.

When your best friend sides with your worst enemy like that, it's enough to make you think you might be wrong. Just because I'm the lead singer, and I write our original material and I (well, Renee and I) figure out the arrangements, and just because I'm the one who got this group together and made us practise until we were really good – not just a bunch of kids messing around on Saturday afternoon – that doesn't mean I'm right all the time.

I guess Renee's not used to having anyone agree with her, because she changed the subject.

'Anyway,' she said, 'we all know it doesn't make any difference what our name is. That isn't why we're not going to play for the dance.'

If she wanted to finish bringing everybody down, she succeeded.

The day before we had tried out, along with some other groups, for the job of playing at the eighth-grade Valentine Mixer. It wasn't a big deal, but it was the first time they had decided to use a group from the school, and it was our first chance to play for a real audience. We'd even get paid. We practised until we were ready to scream, and then I made us practise some more. At the try-out, I thought it had really paid off. Maybe some of the other groups had as much talent – maybe – but we were *together*. I mean you could tell those other groups just jammed with their guitars on Saturday afternoons.

'Everybody knows why we didn't get it,' said Caroline.

The only thing about Caroline is that you have to say Caro*line*, not Carol or Carolinn or anything. She isn't really that kind of person, but her mother is.

'The mixer committee is mostly girls, and Scott is the cutest boy in the school, so of course they picked his group.'

'That isn't what Scott said,' I told them.

'Well, of course he couldn't say that,' Jan said. 'It would sound like he was bragging.'

She really meant it. If anyone except my best friend had told me that Scott Bailey was worried about being modest, I would have given that person a glance of withering scorn. But like I said, Jan can't help being that way.

'What he told me was that we should stop working so hard because nobody wants to listen to a bunch of girls anyway.'

'He's right,' said Renee.

I hope that some day Renee and Scott Bailey get married and have a lot of horrible children who sneer at them.

As a matter of fact, what he actually said was, 'Give up, sweetheart.' He calls all the girls that. He considers it part of his devastating charm. 'Nobody wants to listen to a bunch of girls. But we need a lead singer. If you could fix yourself up to look more like a girl, we could use you.'

I was very polite and self-controlled. I simply told him that I didn't want to work with a bunch of jive turkey amateurs. I won't write down what he said, but I sure hope he and Renee get married some day.

But the thing was, he was right and Renee was right, and we all knew it. No matter how good we were, nobody was going to give us a chance. Right then we were ready to give up. I could feel it. One part of me was looking for a way to keep us together, and the other part wanted to give up along with everybody else.

Then Renee suddenly sat up straight in my special chair, where she had been sprawling all over and crushing my lucky teddy bear.

'Hey, I have an idea!' she said, in this super-cheerful, non-Renee kind of voice.

We all looked up hopefully.

'All we have to do is turn into boys.'

Then she laughed her fantastic Renee kind of laugh. Even Jan was mad.

She even hiccupped a little bit, the way she does when she's really upset.

'You know, Renee, sometimes I think you *like* to make people feel bad.'

But only a small part of me was listening to her. Because the rest of me had just had The Idea. And The Idea was this: Why not?

2

Then I said it aloud. 'Why not?'

'Why not what?' said Caroline.

'Why not be an all-boys rock group?'

They just stared at me.

Then Monica said, 'You mean . . . dress up like boys?'

'That's exactly what I mean!'

This was either the worst idea I'd ever had or the best idea I'd ever had. If I could talk the others into it, that would mean it wasn't as crazy as it sounded.

'Look,' I said, trying to stay cool and exercise my Leadership Potential, which my seventh-grade civics teacher said I have a lot of. 'Everybody knows that there are kids our age who are rock musicians, right?'

Silence. Then Jan said, 'Uh, that's right, Tammy.'

She was humouring me. My best friend was humouring me! Renee was looking at me as if I'd just turned into green slime and started oozing down the walls. But it was too late to stop.

'And some of them are really big stars.'

They were looking at each other, trying to decide who would hold me down and who would call the men in the white coats to take me away.

'Well, what have they got that we don't?'

Renee said, 'Do we get three guesses?'

'They're boys!' I answered triumphantly. 'Now does anyone make them take off their clothes on the stage and prove it?'

A sort of giggling hiccup from Jan. More silence from the others, but it was a different kind of silence.

'See, they say they're boys, and they look like boys, so they are boys.'

Caroline said, 'That's just it, Tammy. They look like boys.'

Maybe, just maybe, it was going to work!

'That's it,' I said. 'You know how old people are always saying you can't tell the girls from the boys nowadays?'

'Oh, them,' said Renee. I will say this for her, she sneers at everyone impartially, regardless of age, creed, or colour.

'But the thing is, they're more or less right. About some kids our age, anyway.'

'Well, actually,' said Monica slowly, 'I wasn't too sure about Chris Barnes when he moved here last summer. I used to see this new kid hanging around, wearing jeans and sweat shirts, and I really wasn't sure until I saw him up close and talked to him.'

'Exactly!' Oops, I was yelling.

'And Scott Bailey is almost too pretty to be a boy,' said Caroline.

I decided to let that pass. After all, it did prove my point.

'You see what I mean,' I said. 'With some of the kids maybe the way we know that they're boys or girls is by their names or their clothes or because we've known them since kindergarten or something.'

'But everybody at Swanson knows who we are,' Monica pointed out.

'I'm not talking about playing at Swanson,' I said,

hoping no one would ask me where I was talking about playing. 'And you can't tell by the way we sound, either.'

This time it was a silence of thoughtful agreement.

'Danny Vericelli still sings soprano in the choir at our church,' said Jan. 'Only I promised not to tell.'

'So we won't tell,' I said impatiently.

Jan said, 'I think we should all promise not to tell. We could swear a vow.'

Best friend or not best friend, Jan does have this romantic streak. She also has trouble sticking to the point.

Just when I was afraid we were going to get side-tracked by this vow, Renee spoke up.

'If this idea works,' she said – was I hearing right? 'If this idea works, we're going to have a lot more than that not to tell.'

Victory.

'And the first thing to decide,' she said – whose idea was this, anyway? – 'is not about Chris Barnes or Scott Bailey, but us. Could we pass for boys?'

We looked at each other.

Then Jan got up and opened the door into the bathroom and stared at herself in the full-length mirror. After a while she came back and sat down, I went and looked at myself next, and then the others went, one by one.

This is what we saw:

Me, Tammy – five feet exactly, ninety-five pounds. Hair short, down around my ears, wavy, and dark brown. Greenish brown eyes. A few freckles, but no pimples, at least not yet. Not completely flat-chested, but nothing one of those baggy shirts couldn't hide. I don't know if you remember what Scott said about my looking more like a girl, but I sure remember. Maybe that was what gave me the idea.

Suppose I'm looking at this person standing before me in the mirror, and someone says, 'I'd like you to meet Tommy.' Yes, I think I'd see a boy, because they'd say, 'Tommy', and right away I'd *know* it was a boy.

Weird.

Jan – four feet ten, ninety pounds. Big blue-grey eyes with long lashes. Come to think of it, my brother Steve has long curly eyelashes. My grandmother is always talking about them. 'Such a shame they're wasted on a boy,' she says, and then looks at me. Maybe my grandmother should marry Scott Bailey.

As for the rest of her, Jan has medium-length dark blond hair – lots of boys in our class have that – thin lips, no figure a loose shirt wouldn't hide. No, the problem with Jan isn't her looks, it's her personality. She's – well, she's just too nice to be a boy. I think that is what my father calls reverse sexism, but I don't care. It's true.

Renee – five feet four, about a hundred pounds. Dark hair in a pony tail, olive complexion, and grey eyes. The fact is, Renee looks a lot like Mick Jagger. My mother says that when she grows out of those pimples she will be quite striking, whatever that means. Anyway, no problem with Renee.

Monica – five feet one, one hundred pounds. Monica is black, or says she is. Actually, she is a creamy brown, but she explained to me that she is black because she says she's black and she feels black. I asked her did that mean I could be black if I said I was black. Renee isn't the only one who can sneer.

Monica has ripply black hair, which she wears in a long braid down her back. A cute figure, but no serious problem. There's something about her face, though. And I don't know any boys in our class who wear their hair that long.

Caroline – five feet one, 105 pounds. Short, curly blond hair, brown eyes, fair skin. A definite problem here.

Caroline was the last one to go to the mirror. She also stayed the longest. Finally she said, 'The fact is, I look like a girl.' She didn't sound very sorry about it.

'Almost too pretty to be a boy,' Renee said.

Caroline didn't seem to think that was very funny, so I quickly brought us back to the point.

'Even you,' I pointed out, 'can look like a boy if you really want to.'

'But –' I had to cut her off fast. Caroline wasn't the only one who didn't really want to.

'Caroline,' I said sternly, 'we all know that you are the cutest girl in the eighth grade.' It was no time to beat around the bush. 'Did that get us a chance to play for the Valentine Mixer?'

She shook her head.

'When we are playing together on the stand, you can be a girl or you can be a drummer. You have to choose. You can be a girl the rest of the time.'

Everyone brightened up at that thought, even me.

'But what about my hair?' said Monica.

'You're right,' I said. 'It makes you look like a girl or a hippie or something. You'll have to cut it.'

Monica looked stubborn. 'I can't,' she said. 'It won't go into an Afro, and that's the only way I'll wear my hair short.'

Inspiration. 'A wig,' I said, 'an Afro wig.'

I got my first really enthusiastic response.

'Wow! An Afro wig! Then I'll really look black.'

'Right on,' I said.

Back in the sixth grade I did a book report on a biography of Napoleon. I've always remembered one sentence I read: 'He was born to be a leader of men.' I liked the way that sounded. And that's the way I felt right then. Come to think of it, Napoleon had nothing on me. I'd like to see him persuade the whole French army to dress up like girls.

3

In school, you think you know what's going to be hard and what's going to be easy, and ninety per cent of the time you're right. The other ten per cent is what keeps school from being completely boring, as far as I'm concerned. But life, or show business anyway, is different.

To convince everyone that my idea would work, I had to get us a job, and I knew of one. There's another junior high in Rocky Point. Adams is where the rich kids go. It's a public school like ours, but smaller and out by the Point. The neighbourhood is so exclusive there's no need for kids to go to a private school. In fact, my cousin Lottie, who goes there, told me that her parents were thinking of sending her to boarding school next year because it would be more democratic. She had also told me that Miss Michaels, the Social Activities Director, was grousing about how hard it was to find a band to play for their Spring Hop.

I figured out all the angles, which is what leaders are for, and Monday afternoon I went to a phone booth, looked up the number, called Adams, and asked for Miss Michaels.

'Yes?'

'I heard that you're looking for a group to play for the spring dance you're having, and I've got one.'

'What's the name of your group?'

'Tommy and the Tigers.' I'd talk to the others about

that later. The important thing was that we had to have a name, and that one sounded OK to me.

'You sound young.'

'We are,' I said. 'We're in eighth grade, but we have experience. Mostly we play for private parties, but we'd like to –'

'How much?'

Here was the big one. Too little and she'd laugh; too much and she'd turn us down. I closed my eyes, held my breath, and said: 'Fifty dollars.'

'You're hired.'

I had to lean against the side of the phone booth. I saw stars, our names in lights. Fortunately, I still had the receiver next to my ear.

'Tommy? Are you there? This is Tommy I'm speaking with?'

'Uh, yeah.'

'April fifteenth at eight. I'll need your last name and your phone number, so we can be in touch about the details.'

I made a crash landing. Figured out all the angles, had I?

'As a matter of fact, my brother, my older brother, Steve Ballantyne, he's – uh – like our manager really, I mean we're just kids, I only called you because –'

'What's the number?'

I gave her his. Mine. Ours.

I did not panic. Maybe I did hurry a little, going home, but by the time I got there I was able to breathe normally. I asked casually, 'Is Steve here?'

Mom looked surprised. In the first place, he was never home these days except for meals, and in the second place, the last time I'd expressed any interest in him I was about ten. She shrugged.

'Not yet. He'll be back for dinner, or at least he'd better be, since I'm only making this for the two of you.'

They were going out to a dinner party.

An incredible opportunity – they go to about four dinner parties a year.

I put it off, deciding that it would be better to tackle him after he'd been fed.

I don't remember ever eating a meal that lasted so long, but Steve finally finished eating, gave me a funny look when I volunteered to do the dishes, and went up to his room.

While I did the dishes, I thought about him more than I'd needed to for a while. I had adored Steve until I was five and figured out that he'd always be five years older than me, that I'd never catch up. I could have killed him. In fact I tried to several times, but it always ended up with us getting sent to our rooms.

He's a freshman in college, and these days he seems almost more like a grown-up; not that I ever admit it when he tries to pull rank on me. But I've compared him with other people's older brothers, and he really could pass for a junior or senior. Maybe he picked it up at the chess club he belongs to at the state college campus, about twenty miles from here. This really impresses some people, my parents for instance. It doesn't impress me – two years ago he decided he needed someone to practise on and showed me the rules, and we played. The first game was a draw, and the second game I beat him. He got into a huff and didn't want to play anymore, which was fine with me; it's a boring game. Right now I just hoped he wasn't still holding a grudge.

What impressed *me* about the chess club was the way Steve used it when he was talking Mom and Dad into buying that van of his. It was a used one, and he'd already saved up a third of the price from his allowance and his part-time job, and most of what he makes now goes into paying them back. The point was, what did he need it for? That weekly commute to the chess club was the clincher. Steve is a smooth operator. He also gets almost all A's without studying nearly as hard as I do, so I've always had the feeling that maybe he isn't just older than me, but smarter, too.

Since he got the van, he hasn't even been home that much of the time, what with his part-time job, and the fact that he can do his homework in five minutes, and — well, he claims he spends his evenings at the library, and with his grades who could disprove it? For that matter, who cares?

Only now I needed him. I needed his brains, and I needed that van.

The door to his room was a little open. I peeked in, and he was at his desk, studying for once. Studying hard, it looked like. Not exactly in the mood for an interruption. Oh well, now or never.

I pushed the door open a little wider.

'Steve?'

He jumped like he'd been shot, pushed whatever he'd been studying into a desk drawer, and looked around.

'Yeah?'

'I need a favour. Kind of a big one.'

'And what may that be, Sister Dear?'

I *hate* it when he calls me that. I took a deep breath. Napoleon, I told myself, got where he did by pretending he didn't mind an insult and getting even later. But how he *really* got there, I decided, was by following his instincts, so I followed mine, and just said:

'Actually I do hate it when you call me that. I wish you wouldn't.'

Steve turned all the way around, and grinned at me.

'I bet that's not the favour you need.'

I grinned back.

'I bet you're right.'

He jerked his head in the way that means 'Come in,' and said: 'What is it?'

I went in, sat down on the bed, and braced myself. The first part of this was going to be the worst. Of course, it might also be the last part.

'You know this group that I have – I mean that I play with?'

'How could I not? That basement isn't exactly soundproof.'

I swallowed hard, fixed my eyes on the floor, and told him about our problem and the way we'd decided to solve it. Then I waited for him to laugh or throw me out.

He just said: 'And?'

'And it worked. We have a job on April fifteenth, only it's playing for a junior high dance all the way across town, and we'll have to have transportation or nobody's parents will let us, including Mom and Dad, and I got us the job over the phone, see, and she had to have a number to call back and I couldn't give her mine only I did but what I really couldn't give her was my name, so —'

'So you gave her mine.'

'Yeah. I told her —'

'I'm supposed to be your manager, right?'

At least he catches on fast. I finally looked up at him.

'Please? Just this once?'

Steve was leaning back with his arms behind his head, which he does when he's thinking. A good sign. But what he said was:

'I have a date that night.'

'She could come along.' I was desperate.

'To a junior high dance? Be serious.'

Well, no one could say I hadn't tried. Pull yourself together, Tammy, and get yourself out of this room before you start to cry.

Steve sat forward.

'A chess tournament,' he said.

'What chess tournament?' I mumbled.

'The one on April fifteenth. The one I have to break my date for. I presume you don't want this little plan of yours spread all over town.'

'No!' I shrieked. 'I mean, is this yes, are you saying yes?'

'Yes, I'm saying yes.'

'You'll really do it?'

'That's the idea.'

I sat there, so limp and light-headed with relief I wasn't sure I had the strength to move.

'You know,' Steve said, 'any normal little sister would be throwing her arms around my neck and saying "How can I ever thank you?" or words to that effect.'

As I got unsteadily to my feet he said, 'Never mind, Sister Dear. These things have to be spontaneous.'

'I wasn't –'

'Now, you've got to give me this woman's name and phone number, so I can make the arrangements.'

'Miss Michaels. I'll go get them.'

When I got to the door I turned and said, 'Thank you, Brother Dear.'

Why had it been so easy? I knew I wasn't about to get something out of Steve for nothing. But I was so relieved just then, I decided to worry about that later.

4

My family is OK. I'd give them about a B. Sometimes a B−, sometimes a B+. Although, I have to give them an A, especially my mother, for letting us do all our rehearsing in the rumpus room. It does get pretty loud sometimes.

I had to do some convincing to get my parents to buy me an electric guitar. It was different for Caroline. Her mother is liberated. Personally, I think she gets carried away by the whole thing, but I'm sort of sorry for her, feeling the way she does and having a daughter like Caroline, who is very feminine and popular with boys. Maybe I should feel sorry for Caroline, being the way she is and having a mother like that, but it's hard to feel sorry for Caroline.

Anyway, Caroline's mother got her a great set of used drums for Christmas to toughen her up or something, and Caroline found out she really liked drumming. That's how she came to join the group. Those drums gave me the idea of having a real group, instead of just messing around after school.

Renee sneers a lot about her family, but they sound like a solid C to me. On the other hand, when I asked her how she got them to shell out for that really fabulous guitar with the terrific amplifiers, she shrugged and said, 'I just asked them.' So I figure that rates at least a B. It isn't just her guitar, though. Renee is really good. She's our lead guitar and probably the most talented person in the group, even including me.

But then I have a lot of other things going for me.

Monica's electric bass belongs to her older brother, who lets her use it while he's away at college.

Jan backs me up on the vocals and plays tambourine or whatever else we need. Sometimes we all sing.

Wednesday, when we all met for our next session in the rumpus room, Caroline was so full of questions (like what would we wear, what would we tell our parents, how were we going to convince a whole school full of kids who knew us that we were boys) that I was glad I'd done what I'd done.

'Aha!' I said.

Jan looked worried.

'We are not going to convince a whole school full of kids who know us. We are going to convince a whole school full of kids who *don't* know us – at Adams.'

'Adams Junior High?' squeaked Jan.

'Adams Junior High,' I said. 'I called them up about their Spring Hop. It's in six weeks, and we're going to play for it.'

At the same time, Caroline said, 'Who's going to play for it?' and Monica said, 'How did you . . .'

'Tommy and the Tigers are going to play for it,' I said. 'And the way we got the job,' I admitted, 'is that we were so cheap. They don't have a committee the way we do at Swanson. I talked to this teacher who's Social Activities Director for this semester. She sounded pretty bored by the whole thing, and she said everybody else wanted too much, so I said we'd do it for fifty dollars.'

'They're going to *pay* us,' Jan breathed.

Everybody looked impressed except Guess Who, who of course was about to point out how much that came to apiece. I continued quickly.

'I know it's not much,' I said, sounding as modest and apologetic as I could, 'but it's a real job, and if we're a hit, we can charge more later.'

Renee found something else to sneer at.

'Tommy and the Tigers,' she said, but even she couldn't make it sound that bad. 'You're Tommy, I suppose.'

'Well, uh, yeah. I mean, it sounds like my real name and everything . . .' I trailed off because I suddenly felt very strange. Giving myself an actual boy's name. It felt kind of creepy. I had to remind myself that there was no way I could actually turn into a boy. Our school is very modern about sex education; as a matter of fact, they are always telling us a lot more than I, personally, want to know. If anything like that could happen, I'm sure they would have told us about it.

But Caroline was asking, 'Didn't she say anything? About the way you sounded, or were you a boy or a girl?'

'No, she just said I sounded young. So I told her it was OK, we have experience and everything. See, we don't have to convince anyone. It never occurred to her that I might be a girl.'

'Well . . .' said Monica slowly, and I could tell that this was the first time the plan had seemed real to her.

'Who's going to drive us over there with all our equipment?' Caroline asked.

The Born Leader is always prepared.

'Our parents already know about the group,' I

pointed out. 'We could just tell them about playing over at Adams, that's all they need to know. And my brother Steve is going to drive us over in his van.'

'Does he know?' asked Caroline.

'I had to tell him, because I had to leave our number for that teacher, to let her know where she could reach me. If she calls about something and asks for Tommy . . . So I told her to ask for Steve, that he was . . . like our manager. He said it sounded crazy to him, but he'd do it.'

'It sounds crazy to me,' said Caroline, 'but as long as you said we'd do it, I guess we better do it, at least this time.'

Some gratitude. And we were even getting paid.

'But do we all have to have boys' names?' asked Monica.

'I think we'd better, just in case,' said Renee. 'And we can practise calling each other by them when we're by ourselves.'

'Well, I can't pick out a boy's name just like that,' said Jan.

'We can each think of one tonight and tell them tomorrow,' said Caroline.

Once everybody gets interested in your plan, it's not exactly all yours anymore.

'The main thing is, what are we going to wear?' said Caroline. For Caroline that is always the main thing, but this time she had a point.

Everybody agreed with me about the baggy shirts, and we decided on black jeans and black boots.

Monica had a real inspiration. 'When I was downtown Saturday,' she said, 'I saw some sort of thick cotton material with a tiger-stripe pattern. We could make waist-coats to wear over our shirts. That would go with our name, and if we made them with straight sides to reach to our hips, it would help to sort of de-emphasize our figures, and –'

'And it would look terrific,' said Caroline. 'Just because we're going to be boys doesn't mean we can't look good.'

That's Caroline for you. Even if she's got to look like a boy, she wants to look good. On the other hand, if you had told me two days before that I would ever see Caroline enthusiastic about something that de-emphasized her figure, I would have laughed at you.

5

Everyone except Monica and Caroline picked a name that sounded like her real one. Renee was Ron, Jan was Jim. I pointed out that Jan could be a boy's name, but Jan said she was taking no chances that anyone would even wonder, like with Chris Barnes.

Monica announced that her name was going to be Sebastian.

'Sebastian!?' we all said, more or less at once.

'Yes,' said Monica stubbornly. 'In fact, my name is Sebastian Fox.'

'But we don't need last names,' said Jan. 'Do we?' She looked at me anxiously.

'No,' I said firmly. 'But as long as we don't have to call you Mr Fox or something, I guess you can be Sebastian Fox. Only, if I introduce you that way, people might start wondering about the rest of our last names, and we don't want that.'

It seems incredible to me now that not one of us realized what we were getting ourselves into. Blind, that's what we were.

So Monica agreed to just sort of *be* Sebastian Fox, Sebastian for short.

Then Caroline said that her name was going to be George.

We just looked at her.

Jan said, 'Is that your father's name or something?'

'No,' said Caroline. 'It's not my father's name or my

uncle's name or anything like that. Once I had a cat named George.'

While the rest of us were thinking that over, Renee said briskly, 'George it is. Let's set up and start rehearsing and practise calling each other by our boys' names.'

Oh well, a Born Leader need a good second-in-command. Sometimes.

By the end of the afternoon, I was glad we had six weeks to work on this, including spring vacation. Not because of our playing, but because of the names. We couldn't seem to say them without laughing. Especially Caroline's. Finally, when it was time for Caroline to do her special drum solo, Renee yelled, 'Take it, George!' and all of us except Caroline collapsed into a giggling shambles. She just sat there with a stony expression on her face, but I still couldn't stop laughing. Nobody could.

When it had all died down, even the last hiccup from Jan, Caroline spoke.

'That cat I told you about was a kitten I got when I was six years old. And I named it George, because I thought George was the most beautiful name in the world, only later it turned out to be a her, not a him. And Mother wouldn't let me call her George anymore. I had to call her Georgette or some stupid name like that. So after that I didn't call her anything, except when we were alone. But it wasn't the same — I mean George just being her name when we were alone. It wasn't really her name anymore.

'Tammy, you said that when I'm being a drummer I have to be a boy. Well, I will, and my name is going to be George.'

'OK by me, George,' I said. And I didn't even feel like laughing. After that it was easier.

But it made me see a problem that I brought up with the others after the session.

'About this giggling,' I said. 'That's something girls do and boys don't.'

'Boys giggle sometimes,' said Jan.

'But only when something is really funny,' said Caroline, 'or when they hear a really dirty joke.'

'Renee hardly ever giggles,' said Monica.

'But that's part of being at school,' said Caroline. 'You know, when you're standing around with some other girls in the hall, and some boy you like goes by, or a teacher you've just been talking about, of course you all giggle. If we stopped giggling at school, people would think there was something weird about us.'

'Like they do about me,' said Renee.

A *very* uncomfortable silence.

Say something, Tammy. Anything. 'Well,' I improvised, 'I guess we could practise not giggling while we're talking to each other on the phone and at rehearsals. At school, well, we'll try to involve ourselves in non-giggling situations.'

Then we all started to laugh, even Renee.

Usually when I say something that isn't supposed to be funny but turns out that way, I hate it. But this time it turned out to be exactly the right thing to do. Leadership is very tricky.

Getting used to our names was harder than we thought. Not because they were boys' names, but because they weren't ours.

We discovered that there's only one name in the world you react to in a certain way, and that's your own. If your name was, say, Kathy, and you decided to change it to Bonnie, the first time someone said, 'Hi, Bonnie', you wouldn't look up right away. Or the next few hundred times, either.

When we were alone together we used nothing but our stage names. At first we made a lot of mistakes – 'Hey, Mon – uh, I mean Sebastian' – but as time went on we got a lot smoother.

Of course, it took a while because at school or when other people were around we had to use our real names. Once at school I called Caroline 'George'. It just slipped out. Talk about giggling! But it was OK, because girls at school are always laughing about some kind of silly secret joke, so no one really noticed.

One good thing about having six weeks was that it gave Caroline/George's hair time to grow.

I know it sounds strange to grow your hair longer to look like a boy, but that's how it turned out.

The look for boy rock stars that year was smooth, shoulder-length hair, and that's what we decided we should all have, except for Monica. She insisted on wearing her Michael Jackson wig every time we practised. Anyway, I know a boy can have short, curly hair, but on Caroline it looked very girlish. So she agreed to grow it longer and to straighten it a little for the show. Meanwhile, she started wearing it in two pony tails and looked just as cute as ever.

For some reason, I started finding ways of doing my own hair to look kind of cute and feminine.

Caroline went to our Valentine Mixer with some

boy from the football team. Jan went with Danny Vericelli, the boy from the choir.

The King of the Creeps had the nerve to ask me to go with him! 'Of course, I won't have much time to dance,' Scott said. 'But we might let you sit in on a couple of numbers. I like your hair that way.'

I was so mad I couldn't think of anything to say except No.

I was going to shave my head, but Renee pointed out that there are no bald-headed teenage rock stars.

'You know, Tommy,' said Caroline thoughtfully the next afternoon, when we were practising in the rumpus room, 'I think Scott really likes you.'

For someone who is supposed to know so much about boys, Caroline can be pretty dumb.

Anyway, she reported that Scott's group didn't play nearly as well as we did, which was good, and that everybody loved them anyway, which was also good, I decided, because that meant that as boys we would be playing twice as well as we needed to.

I pointed this out to the group because we needed all the encouragement I could think of. You see, that was the bad part about having these six weeks. It gave us all time to think about what a weird idea it was and to wonder if we should call it off.

A Born Leader does not discuss her doubts with her people. Especially when they're all feeling even more doubtful than she is. Except for Renee, that is. She was very calm about the whole thing, and that helped the rest of us. If the most pessimistic person in the whole group thought we could get away with it, then maybe we had a chance.

But Renee is not the kind of person you take your problems to, so I talked to Steve. He was the closest thing to a grown-up who knew about this, and if he said we should call it off, then maybe we should.

About a week before the Spring Hop at Adams, I talked to him.

'Oh, no you don't,' he said. 'I don't know if this crazy stunt will work, but I have to see how it comes out. Anyway, I talked to that teacher over at Adams, and she sounds kind of cute.'

'Steve!' I said. 'She's a *teacher*! And you're only a college freshman!'

'But she's only a junior high school teacher,' he pointed out.

I knew there was something wrong with his logic, but this was no time to bring it up. So much depended on him.

Transportation, of course. But, also, everybody's parents knew that we were going to play at another school, at night. They all called up my mother, who explained that Steve would take care of us and assured them that he was very reliable for his age, and things like that. So that was all right.

And finally it came. The Night.

6

I washed my hair, and after I got dressed I smoothed it out with the dryer. I even borrowed Mom's hair spray so it would stay smooth.

I went to the full-length mirror to see if I looked like a boy, but all I could see was that I looked pretty good. Boy/girl-wise, I didn't look very much one way or the other.

Now for the first tricky part. Steve was waiting for me so we could go pick up the others. On an occasion like this there was no way to get out of going to show myself to my parents. Of course they would want to see me dressed up for my first real performance.

I went into the living room where they were watching TV. My mother said, 'You look very nice, dear,' which is what she says automatically if my hair is combed and my fingernails are clean. Then she and Dad got this puzzled expression on their faces and looked at each other the way people do when they are trying not to look at each other.

I once saw a picture of my mom dressed for her Senior Prom, and she was wearing lots of ruffles and lace and net. That's what someone would have worn in those days who was going to sing at a dance. Mom and Dad knew that wasn't what a girl would wear now, but they didn't know what she *would* wear. Of course a girl who wanted to look like a girl wouldn't wear what I was wearing, but they didn't know that. If you want to hear the they-all-look-alike-these-days number, you should hear my father sometime.

No one spoke for a minute, and then my father said, 'As a matter of fact, Tammy, you do look nice.' I think he really meant it, too.

All the others got the same reaction from their families, I learned, later except Renee; her parents were out.

Steve and I loaded up my equipment and we were off. We picked Caroline up first, because she lived nearest. She was all dressed and smooth-haired, and looked pretty convincing if you didn't know; but on the way to Jan's she said, 'I just read about this group that has a girl drummer.'

'Not a girl drummer named George,' Steve said.

Caroline flashed me a reproachful glance, so I pointed out that our manager had to know our stage names.

Renee had cut her hair, and she looked great. She made a much better looking boy than she did a girl.

Monica put her wig on in the car. That wig really did make a difference. It made her whole face look more boyish.

In fact, the only problem was Jan. She looked OK, I thought. (It's *very* hard to tell if someone looks like a boy when you know she's a girl.) But her eyes were like saucers. Maybe boys feel that scared sometimes, but they never look it.

Steve turned out to be a pretty good manager. He made me get out so that Jan could sit beside him on the front seat, and on the way to Adams he talked and made jokes as if the whole thing weren't that important. Any other time that would have made me mad, but I was sitting next to Jan on the other side, and I could feel her relaxing – sort of.

And then there we were, and Steve was parking the van, and this woman was walking towards us, who must be the Social Activities Director I'd talked to. She was pretty young for a teacher. Jan suddenly went rigid.

'The bathroom!' she gasped. 'How do we go to the bathroom? Which one . . .'

We all froze, except Steve. And of course, we all needed to go to the bathroom right then. Badly.

But Steve was out of the van and talking to Miss Michaels about setting up our equipment in the gym, and where was the Green Room? I found out afterward that the Green Room is the name of a special room where the performers in a show can go and relax. They're the only ones who can use it.

Miss Michaels looked surprised, but she seemed to know what he was talking about.

'Well, um . . .' she said, 'you could use the coach's office. That opens off the gym and it has its own bathroom. I'll go and get the key.'

I asked Steve later if it felt good to have five girls fall in love with you at once, even if they were only junior-high girls and they were disguised as boys and one of them was your sister.

He said that it did.

7

You should definitely be young and healthy to try this kind of thing. Anyone over twenty would have had at least three heart attacks going through what we went through that night. And the first one would have happened when Miss Michaels smiled at us and said, 'I'm so glad to see you're a mixed group.'

Jan's eyes turned back into saucers. Someone (possibly me) made a sort of strangled squeak. We must have looked like a bunch of rabbits staring at a boa-constrictor. After about two seconds by the clock and several hours by real time, she said, 'It's always nice to see children of different races working together.'

I used every muscle in my body to send out waves of command. Don't giggle. I will kill the first one who giggles. But I managed to unclench my jaw enough to mutter, 'Uh, thank you, ma'am. Steve and, uh, Ron, here, will be setting up the equipment, and the rest of us – if you could show us the, uh, Green Room – we'll, uh, we'll be running over our songs.'

As speeches go, it wasn't the Gettysburg Address, but it did get us away from Miss Michaels and into the coach's office, where we collapsed in hysterics. Jan got the hiccups again and we had to thump her on the back.

Renee was still out there with Steve and Miss Michaels, but she looks more like a boy than any of us and actually has a lot of cool for someone our age, so I wasn't too worried.

By the time we had calmed down, we could hear that some kids were there already. It was almost time to start. We were combing our hair one more time and collecting our tambourines and stuff when Caroline froze.

'Tammy,' she whispered. 'Tammy, we're going to go out on a lighted platform, in front of about a thousand kids, and pretend we're *boys*?'

The Born Leader knows that panic is contagious. At that moment, it was contaging right before my eyes. In fact it is so contagious that I was surprised that I could still open my mouth to speak.

'Caroline,' I said, slowly and clearly, 'we are not pretending anything. We have never told anyone that we are boys. All we did was change our names for show business, which lots of people do. We are going to go out there and play music just the way we always do. We are going to be ourselves. We're not trying to fool anyone. We're just letting them think whatever they want to see? Now let's go.'

That was a good speech. It kept the others so busy trying to figure out if it made sense or not that they were distracted from being scared.

And the next thing we knew we were out there doing our thing, and the kids were doing their thing, and nobody was staring or pointing or anything. And we knew it was going to be all right.

The one thing we weren't pretending about was that we were musicians. (That speech was a bunch of baloney, of course. All good speeches are. Ask any Born Leader.) The only difference it made was that after the first number, we played extra well just from being so relieved.

The kids seemed to like us. They clapped like mad at the end of the first half, when we headed for the Green Room.

During the intermission, I decided to see if I could find Steve. I really wanted to find out what the kids were thinking.

I was skulking along the hall outside the gym, when I heard two girls talking.

One of them said, 'And they're so darling.'

The other one said, 'Yeah, especially that tall one with the dark hair. Do you think that's Tommy?'

The first one said, 'No, Tommy is the short one who does most of the singing.' (The short one?) 'The one you mean is called Ron; I heard the drummer call him that.' Thank God for all our practice with names.

The second girl said, 'Ron,' kind of thoughtfully. 'That's a nice name.'

I was thinking I should pass that on to Renee when she said, 'And he's so sexy.' Hmmm, should I pass that on to Renee?

The first one said, 'Yeah. It's the way he never smiles.'

That's true about Renee. She doesn't smile very often unless you count sneering. On stage she hardly ever smiles at all. If she didn't play so well, I wouldn't have wanted her in the group. You're supposed to smile. But apparently if you're a boy it's OK not to smile.

Then the other one said, 'I wonder where they're from. Maybe they're from Swanson.'

I am young and healthy, so I did not have a heart attack. But it's true what they say about a person's blood running cold.

It happens.

8

We were all really quiet going home. I don't know if it was because there was nothing to talk about or too much to talk about. We had done it. We had played for a bunch of kids and they had really liked it. It wasn't at all like playing for your family and friends. These were strangers. (Except I did see my cousin Lottie's best friend. She looked right at me and didn't bat an eyelash.) So they didn't *have* to like it. And we had even been paid!

Another thing was that they had sort of – well, looked up to us, a little bit. Even though we were just kids their own age, we were The Band.

I guess Renee was quiet because she couldn't think of a discouraging word at first, but after a while she thought of one and spoke up.

'Ten dollars apiece,' she sneered. 'That's just about enough for new guitar strings.'

'Not ten dollars apiece,' said Steve. 'Eight. I'm keeping ten for my commission. After all, I'm your manager.'

'That's twenty per cent,' said Caroline. 'Managers are supposed to get ten per cent.'

That was interesting because usually when she's around a boy Caroline will not admit that she can add two and two; but I guess Steve was so much older that he didn't count. And besides, it was her money.

All Steve said was, 'You want to get another manager?'

(So that was it! I wasn't terribly surprised. In fact, I felt relieved when he said that, because now I knew what he was after. And as I pointed out to the others the next day, it wasn't really a rip off because Steve had special problems that most managers of rock groups don't have. As things turned out, that was an understatement.)

Jan hadn't even been listening. Her eyes were shining and she was glowing quietly.

'They really liked us!' she said. 'And we didn't even know them!'

'Well, they sure didn't know us,' said Monica.

That did it. We had to suspend the no giggling rule again, even Renee.

Mom and Dad were waiting up, of course, and I must have looked pretty serious when we came in. Mom said, 'Did everything go all right, dear?' I managed to say 'Fine' before I exploded again and had to race upstairs holding my hand over my mouth and giggling through my nose.

Just before I got to my room I heard Steve say, 'No, it's OK. Everything went all right. It's just the excitement.'

As far as I was concerned, he was worth his weight in twenty per cents.

The next day when we got together we all talked a mile a minute about everything, and everyone said things like, 'We did it! We really did it!' The Born Leader knows that when people stop saying 'You got me into this' and start saying 'We did it', that is actually a good sign, even if it is kind of irritating.

But then Jan said, 'It was Tammy's idea to begin

with.' She is very loyal. She is also very idealistic, which is not always such a good thing.

Jan continued, 'The thing is that they really liked us, and they didn't necessarily know we were boys. Like you said last night, Tammy, we didn't say we were boys, so maybe we don't have to pretend at all.'

Everybody looked at me. I didn't look at anyone. I still hadn't decided whether to tell about that conversation I had overheard in the hall.

'They think we're boys, all right,' I said finally. 'I heard these two girls talking and they – they think we're boys.'

'How do you know?' said Monica.

'Yeah,' said Renee. 'Did one girl walk up to the other girl and say, "I think those are boys"?'

I hate it when people are sarcastic.

'Well, no,' I admitted. 'They were just saying – well, how cute we were.'

Silence while everyone thought about that. I had already had plenty of time to think about it, so I told them what I had figured out.

'If you're a girl, and you see a boy your own age or a little older, the first thing you notice is how good-looking he is, right? Even if you don't care too much about things like that, you can't help noticing. So these people, who were girls, were looking at these other people, who were boys (I mean, that's what they thought), so naturally they noticed whether we were good-looking or not. That's all. The boys there probably didn't even look at us.'

'That's weird,' said Caroline.

'It *is* kind of creepy,' I admitted. 'But remember why

Scott Bailey got to play for the dance at Swanson? It wasn't just because he was a boy; it was because he was a neat-looking boy – I mean,' I corrected myself hastily, '*some* people think so, anyway. So we should be glad that people think we look like cute boys, because that's part of the job; people who perform on a stage are supposed to be good-looking.'

There was an awkward silence in the room, until Jan, good ol' Jan, finally said, 'Well, I guess we better just go on as we are.'

'Right,' I said briskly. 'I don't know where our next job is going to come from, but I'll find something. It's too late to start practising this afternoon, but tomorrow we're going to start working on a new number. An original.'

'What's it called?' said Renee.

'Well,' I said, 'remember "Danny Darling"?'

Everybody groaned except Renee who pretended to throw up, which I think is very childish.

'Danny Darling' was the name of this song I wrote – the only one that I ever made up entirely, words and music – and it was really dumb. I wrote it when we were the Teenettes, and it was supposed to sound nostalgic, but actually it just sounded sappy.

Even Jan agreed, although it was Renee who called it that.

'No,' I said, 'wait, I've changed it and speeded it up, and now it's called "Didi Darling".'

'Why did you change the name?' asked Jan.

'Obviously,' said Caroline, 'if we're supposed to be a bunch of boys we can't go around singing a love song about another boy.'

43

Monica got that stubborn look on her face.

'If you think I'm going to get up on a stage and sing a love song about a girl . . .'

'No, no,' I yelled. 'Wait! It's not like that anymore, honest! Let me run through it for you, and we'll vote, OK?'

I plugged in my guitar and did it for them. It really is very cute and fast and bouncy, and everybody said they liked it. Except Renee, who didn't say anything.

Coming from her, that means a lot.

9

It was a good thing everybody liked 'Didi Darling', because we only had a week and a half to learn it. Steve told me Miss Michaels had called. 'It looks like we really were a hit,' he said.

'What do you mean, "we"?'

'If you don't want the job, just say so,' he said. Then I had to say 'We owe everything to our wonderful manager' ten times before he'd tell me about it. The Born Leader knows when to humour other people's childish whims.

This girl at Adams was having a birthday, and her parents were giving a party at the country club for about forty kids. They wanted us to play for it.

'Did you call them up?' I asked.

'Yep,' said Steve. 'I told them eighty bucks.'

'Oh, no!'

'Well, Angela, I mean Miss Michaels, said not to ask for less than a hundred, or they'd think we were no good. But, after all, you are just a bunch of – just a bunch of kids, so I said eighty and Mrs Rensler said yes.'

The others were impressed too. Caroline even stopped complaining about Steve's twenty per cent.

This time there was no problem getting our parents' approval. It was in the daytime, it was a birthday party, and you can't get much more respectable-sounding than the country club.

Apparently, they hadn't heard what we'd heard about some of the after-prom parties the high-school kids had up there, but as I pointed out to the others, this wasn't going to be one of those parties.

'It better not be,' said Caroline.

Mom did look kind of puzzled when I came down all dressed and ready to go. 'Aren't you going to be hot in that outfit?' she asked.

'Well, yes,' I said, 'but we all have to match.'

She seemed satisfied, but that was one more problem to worry about. Suppose we got more jobs this summer? It looked like a hot summer, too. What do boys wear in hot weather? What do boys wear in hot weather that *we* could wear?

That's what we discussed on the way to the party. No one could figure out afterward how we managed not to realize that we had some much bigger problems coming up right now.

While he was parking the van, Steve said, 'I hope you've all got your names straight, and when it comes to bathrooms, you're on your own.'

Hate. Kill.

Mrs Rensler greeted us. Her daughter Deirdre was the birthday girl. Fortunately, she did all the talking and didn't seem to notice that we were tongue-tied. Or maybe she figured we were awe-struck by our opulent surroundings.

It was pretty awe-striking. The whole place oozed money. But I managed to tune in to what she was saying in time to hear that we simply *must* come along to the pool. Deirdre and her little friends were simply *dying* to meet us.

'Uh, thanks, ma'am,' I said. 'That'd be swell.'

And they really were dying to meet us. It was early, so there was just Deirdre and two of her girl friends.

She said, 'I think you boys are just super, especially Ron.'

Jan hiccupped.

This was one bunch of boys that wasn't going to be noted for its dazzling social charm.

Deirdre's best friend brought me a lemonade and said, 'You know, I don't think I've ever met an actual boy from the other side of the tracks before.'

The Born Leader analyses a situation quickly. I had three choices: 1. laugh hysterically; 2. throw myself into the swimming pool; 3. say 'I've never met an actual girl from the other side of the tracks either, and it's very interesting, but I think we'd better go set up our instruments.'

There wasn't really that much to do – they had a good sound hook-up on the lawn, and Steve had most of it done already; but we all managed to look busy for about ten minutes. That was the good news.

The bad news came from Monica, who had been monopolized by Deirdre's mother. Mrs Rensler wanted to show how wonderful and liberal and kind she was. She told Monica that it was marvellous to see Someone Like Him (only, of course, it was someone like her) working to Improve Himself (herself).

'Monica,' I said, 'I know how you must feel, but you had it easy.' Caroline and Jan agreed.

Renee didn't say anything for a while. She was looking sort of greenish, but then she blurted, 'Well, I hope you all enjoyed yourselves, because there's more

47

to come. Mrs Rensler told me she wanted all of us to join them for ice-cream and cake and get to know each other during our break.'

'But we can't,' I said. 'We barely got through ten minutes with just the three of them.'

'Actually,' said Jan, 'that's the way a lot of boys act around girls. You know, very quiet and stupid and scared.'

'What have they got to be scared about?' said Caroline. 'They're not trying to pretend they're —'

'Shut up, George,' said Renee.

Deirdre and her friends had come out to watch us setting up.

10

The nightmare ended when we started playing. We sounded even better than usual.

The kids loved it, which was a good thing, because we went on playing for about forty-five minutes after we were supposed to break for cake and ice-cream, when we knew the nightmare would start again. We couldn't ignore Mrs Rensler's signals forever, and we finally gave up.

Mingling with the guests turned out to be not quite as bad as before. In the first place, we were braced for it. In the second place, there were lots more kids, which made it easier. Most of the ones who were dying to meet us turned out to be girls. That, I decided, was a good thing. Jan was right about how some boys act around girls, but I had no idea, absolutely none, how boys acted around boys. For all I know, they have a whole secret language or something.

Anyway, I was telling these girls how I liked algebra and hated English, since that was the opposite of how I felt and I hoped it would sound more like a boy. I was thinking 'Gee, this isn't so hard,' when one of them said, 'Where do you go to school?'

Remembering Deirdre's best friend, I managed to mumble around my cake that I went to Roosevelt – a school just outside the city limits of our suburb and definitely on the wrong side of the tracks.

'Does Ron go there, too?' asked another one.

'Uh, yeah, sure,' I said.

There seemed to be a lot of interest in Ron, and where was he, I mean she?

I had to pound on the bathroom door for five minutes before Renee would let me in so that I could tell her what school she went to. I even got her to join the party by pointing out that since she went to this awful school, Mrs Rensler was bound to think she was in there shooting up or popping pills or something.

When we came out of the bathroom, I realized that I probably should have let her stay. She was immediately surrounded by Deirdre and five other girls and looked very much like a person who is about to do something desperate.

'Hey, Ron,' I said. 'Let's do our new number for these kids.'

I didn't say it very loud, and the group was scattered all over the lawn, but everyone was back on the stand in about thirty seconds.

Renee had even recovered enough to sneer, 'And which of our big new smash hits are we going to do?'

The Born Leader learns not to expect gratitude. '"Didi Darling",' I said.

I always did think it was sort of a cute number, but after all, I wrote it. These kids really liked it, though. Afterwards, two of them even asked me where they could get the record. They thought it was a real song!

After we finished that one, Mrs Rensler started herding everybody off toward the pool, so that we could pack up our stuff in peace. Then she came back and gushed all over Steve, telling him what a fine bunch of boys we were, and gave him a cheque.

After that she turned to me and said, 'Where would you like me to send the pictures?'

'Pictures?' I whispered.

'The club photographer got quite a few with you boys in them, and I know you'd like to have a souvenir of this wonderful afternoon.'

'Uh, thank you very much, ma'am. You could just send them in care of Steve, here. He's our manager.'

There is nothing to worry about, I told myself. Nobody at Swanson is ever going to see those pictures.

As my eyes were rolling in panic, I noticed that Deirdre had managed to escape from the pool and was standing there looking wistful.

'Hi, Deirdre,' I said.

She gave a small giggle. 'Oh, nobody calls me Deirdre,' she said, 'except my mom.' She moved closer to me and gazed into my eyes. 'You want to know what everyone else calls me?' She didn't wait for an answer. 'Didi. Like your song. Isn't that fantastic?'

'Gee,' I babbled. 'That's quite a coincidence, all right.'

Then the little birthday nerd spoke up:

'Could we have a picture with just Ron and me?'

'Sure, yes, why not?' I almost shrieked. 'That'll be fine, won't it, Ron?'

Renee didn't say anything. She just went and stood beside Didi (actually about a foot away from her). The photographer started fiddling with his camera while Birthday Girl gazed at Renee adoringly.

So the lead guitarist of Tommy and the Tigers had her picture taken with Didi the Dolt while their leader and spokesman stood around saying 'Uh . . .', the second singer hiccupped hysterically, the drummer made strange honking and snorting noises, and the bass player stared fixedly at the sky.

Much as I hated her, I couldn't blame the nerd's mother for muttering something to the photographer about drugs. I considered changing the name of our group to The Drooling Idiots.

Going home, we had a lot of catching up to do about what we'd told people. Nobody except Monica had given any last names, of course. We had all had the sense to be vague about each other, except I'd had to say that Ron and I went to Roosevelt.

Caroline had told them she went to a special school for children who were studying music. Not bad for the spur of the moment.

Monica had told Mrs Rensler that she lived in Harlem and was here in Rocky Point on an exchange programme.

'Very funny,' I said. 'I bet your father would just die laughing.' Monica's father is a corporation lawyer.

'I don't care,' said Monica. 'It was worth it just to see the look on her face.' We agreed that it probably was.

There was a hiccup from the back seat. I had a premonition of disaster.

'Jan,' I said, 'where did you tell them you were from?'

'Swanson,' she said in a small voice.

'What!' shrieked four large voices.

'Well, we're not doing anything wrong, so why should we try to hide, and no one's going to come looking for us, and school's out in a few weeks anyway, and this girl asked me where I went to school and I couldn't think of anything.'

'You've certainly been thinking since then,' I said bitterly. 'I never heard such a string of lame excuses.'

But a best friend is a best friend, so to change the subject I decided to tell them about Didi's real name. Everyone except Renee thought it was funny. In fairness to Mrs Rensler, I must admit that my own mother named me Tamsin. She says that it's a very beautiful and unusual name and that I'll like it when I grow up. We made a deal that I would take her word for that if she would promise never to call me anything but Tammy in front of my friends until further notice.

I'd thought that after the horrors of that afternoon somebody might want to quit, but it turned out that everyone liked the money and the excitement and playing for a real audience.

'And the popularity,' said Caroline.

Renee shot her a look that would kill a small tree. The Born Leader keeps the peace at all times, but how? Especially when she herself is trying not to laugh?

Jan saved the day. With complete innocence, she said, 'Did you notice that, too? I've always had friends and stuff, but I've never felt so popular in my life as I did this afternoon. Are boys just more popular than girls?'

Renee said thoughtfully, 'You know, Jan, that might not be as dumb as it sounds.'

11

I ended up in summer school. The group had been taking up a lot of time, of course, but the only thing that had happened to my grades was a C in algebra.

In any sane family this would not be the end of the world, but my family is not sane. Not about school. Especially since next fall they were starting this new programme – the High Potential Streamlined Learning Module – and I wouldn't get to be in it with a C in algebra.

Personally, as you know, I had other problems on my mind. But the choice turned out to be summer school and an A in algebra or No Group. All I could do was lower my father's grade in parenthood to a C – for the semester.

As I parked myself in a seat in a stuffy-smelling classroom on a perfect June day, I consoled myself with the thought that a Born Leader never has it easy. How right I was. Horrible old Scott Bailey was sliding into a seat across from mine. And there were plenty of empty ones, too.

The first thing he did was explain to me that he was not there because he flunked or anything. In fact, it turned out he was there for pretty much the same reason that I was. But I could hardly turn around and explain that, of course, I wasn't there because I was a dummy either. So I didn't say anything. I didn't care what he thought, anyway.

Then he said, 'I have a friend who goes to Adams.'

I froze. I panicked. Instead of saying something normal, like 'So what?', I flashed him this big phony smile and said, 'Oh really? How interesting.'

Scott looked at me a little funny. 'He was telling me about a rock group that played at their Spring Hop. They're called Tommy and the Tigers.'

'Any good?' I said, trying to sound bored.

'He said they were terrific. But then you wouldn't be interested in a group that just had boys in it, would you?'

I turned a giggle into a cough. 'Actually,' I said, 'we've disbanded.'

'You've quit?' He really sounded sorry, the hypocrite.

'Yeah,' I said nonchalantly. 'We're into macramé now.'

'Gee, Tammy,' he said. 'You girls weren't that bad.'

(Oh, *thank* you, you rotten creep.)

After class was out he walked me down the hall. I mean, what could I do? He was telling me how his dad was a friend of the head of the Recreation Department. They were planning to stage a Midsummer Fling in the Park in July. 'And we'll probably get to play for the kids,' he said.

'Oh, is that how you get your jobs?' I asked, in an innocent voice.

'What's that supposed to mean?'

'Your dad just happens to be buddies with the head of the Rec Department, and you get the job. Just like that.'

'Well, what do you care? They wouldn't hire you

girls even if you were still playing, which you just said you're not.'

'There are other groups,' I said. Inside me, someone was screaming, 'Tammy, shut up!' I ignored her. 'Like this Les and the Leopards, or whatever they're called. It seems to me that the least you could do is have try-outs. Unless you think you'd lose. Now if you'll excuse me, Scott, I really must go.'

Scott had turned really red in the face. He yelled after me, 'All right, you stuck-up smart aleck, we *will* have try-outs. And you'll see who plays better.'

'Fine,' I called back gaily, 'we'll bring our macramé.'

12

'You're crazy,' said Renee.

'But kids from all over the city will be there,' I pleaded. 'Think of the exposure we'll get.'

'That's exactly what we're thinking of,' said Caroline.

If Renee and Caroline were on the same side, I was in trouble. Even Jan wasn't on my side.

'Tammy,' she said, 'kids from Swanson will be there.'

'I've thought about that,' I said, 'and I'm sure they won't recognize us. How will they know it's us, when we have different names and even a different sex?'

'Tammy,' said Monica, 'some of our families will be there.'

'Oh wow. I forgot about that,' I said lamely. 'But look, we may not even get the job.'

'Especially if we don't try out for it in the first place,' said Renee.

'Which we're not going to,' said Monica.

Just then Steve came charging into the rumpus room, looking very pleased with himself. 'Hey, Tigers, guess what your manager has lined up for you.'

'A job in Australia?' said Caroline hopefully.

'Heck no, it's right here in town. They're going to have this –'

'Midsummer Fling in City Park,' said Renee.

'Right,' said Steve. 'And you're going to –'

'No,' said Monica.

'Why not?' said Steve. Everybody told him why not. Steve thought for a minute. Then he said, 'Listen,' and everybody listened. What was his secret?

'You want to go on with this group, don't you?'

Everyone nodded.

'Then you'll have to take some chances.' He made it sound so simple.

'But what about our families?' said Monica. 'I don't know about the rest of you, but my whole family is planning to be there.'

'As a matter of fact, I've been thinking about that,' said Steve.

Who was running this group, anyway? But, of course, I was interested.

'If you want to go on with this, you're going to have to tell them.'

Everyone started to talk at once and then stopped. We all thought for a minute.

'After all, we're not doing anything wrong,' said Jan slowly.

'Not exactly,' said Monica.

'Well, when we get this job lined up,' said Steve, 'I'll get Mom to invite all your parents over here. We'll have a barbecue or something, get them in a good mood, and tell them.'

He sure was good at making things sound easy.

'You mean, *if* we get the job,' said Renee.

Then the Born Leader had to open her big mouth. 'What do you mean *if*,' I yelled exuberantly. 'The only competition is Scott Bailey's group, and if we can't beat them out . . .'

Four people shrieked 'Who?'

Steve said, 'Who's Scott Bailey?'

While the others were explaining to him who Scott was and how big a chance we'd be taking if we auditioned right in the same auditorium with his group, Renee was looking at me. Hard.

In a level voice, she said, 'How did you hear about this job, Tammy?'

'Well, actually,' I said, trying to sound casual, 'Scott told me about it. He's in my class in summer school.'

No way was I going to tell her the rest of it, but she knew.

'So,' she said, 'you talked us into taking this chance of getting found out, just so you could get even with Scott.'

'No,' I protested. 'I admit I tried to, but Steve was the one who actually talked us into it.'

Pretty lame. Renee was really mad at me, and for some reason I minded a lot. She made it sound so tacky. I tried again.

'That was the reason — a part of it, anyway — at the beginning, but then —'

'I know,' said Renee. 'Then you talked yourself into thinking it was something else.'

I felt like I was about to cry, when I realized that the others had all stopped talking, except for Steve.

'I called the Recreation Department,' he was saying, 'and there are two other groups trying out, including Scott's. So I'll figure out an excuse to be late and try out last, and maybe Scott will be gone by then. Don't worry, I'll think of something.'

I wished I could. I sure wasn't feeling very much like a Born Leader.

He thought of something, all right. They held the auditions at Swanson, so he sneaked around to see what they were doing. Just as the second group was finishing, he phoned the school and said we had dropped a rod or something, and we'd be there as soon as we could find another car. Actually, of course, we were parked a block away in the van.

Then we all sneaked around the corner from the auditorium entrance and saw Scott's mother picking up his group in their van. He argued with her a little – I bet he really wanted to stay and see Tommy and the Tigers – but he must have lost the argument, because they all got in and drove away. Heh-heh-heh.

Of course, they were pretty impatient when we got there, but it turned out we had the job sewed up anyway.

The people deciding on the try-outs were from the Recreation Department and the Volunteer Committee for the Midsummer Fling. They had decided to include some kids as judges, since the music all sounded the same to them anyway. One of them was the niece of the chairwoman of the Volunteer Committee.

'Ronnie!' she squealed, when we walked onto the stage to set up.

You guessed it. Deirdre the birthday girl.

'Well,' said one of the grown-ups in that ho-ho-ho way they have, 'it seems one young lady has already heard of this group.'

'Oh, yes,' breathed Deirdre. 'That's Tommy and the Tigers, but Ronnie is the cute one.'

What a break! She didn't say anything about her birthday party; she made it sound like we had fans.

Which we did, I guess. Anyway, Ronnie had a fan.

We got the job. And it was almost as easy as Steve had said it would be.

Going home from the try-out, the van was noisy with cheers, congratulations, and a chorus or two of 'Didi Darling' until Jan said, 'About telling our parents . . .'

She didn't say it very loudly, but everybody heard her.

I cleared my throat. 'Well actually, Steve . . .'

'I explained,' he broke in, 'that we needed to have a meeting of all the parents of the Tigers. Mom is planning a barbecue for a week from this Friday.'

'And did you explain,' asked Monica, lounging in the back seat like Sebastian Fox in person, 'why?'

'Of course not,' he said. 'I think it's only fair to let them all have it at once. But you have to do your own inviting.'

'She's not going to call them?' Monica asked.

Mom had been firm about that. She knew we were up to something, and whatever it was she didn't want to be any more involved than she was already – which, in a way, was plenty, since she was the one who'd assured the other parents that there was nothing to fear as long as steady, reliable Steve was taking care of us.

'No problem,' Caroline said. 'What worries me is how do we tell them once we've got them there.'

Renee yawned. 'Isn't that what our leader is for?'

Wouldn't it be terrible, I thought, if that door you're leaning against slid open and spilled you out into the traffic. What a tragic loss to the musical world.

'How about our manager?' said my very dearest Jan.
'I won't be there,' Steve said, not even bothering to
sound sorry. 'I've got a date.' He actually chuckled.

13

It was three days before our party. Everyone's parents were lined up for the event – or at least I hoped so. Renee still hadn't said anything one way or the other. The next afternoon we had a job playing for a party in Adams territory. Monica's house was a lot closer to it than ours, and for some reason connected with our manager's social life, he decided it would be easier to take all our gear to her house after this rehearsal and store it there overnight. We'd get ourselves to Monica's the next afternoon, and he'd pick us up there. By this time we were all whizzes at packing and unpacking. The rest of the equipment was in the van, but Renee was still tinkering with an amplifier that she said wasn't working quite right. No one else could hear anything wrong, but nobody questions her judgement about things like that. Steve said he'd take the rest of the stuff and drop the others off, then come back for Renee and her equipment.

That left the two of us.

'Uh, Renee?' I said.

She didn't look up from whatever she was doing to the amplifier.

'My mother's busy she can't make it.' She said that like it was all one word.

'Well, why didn't you –' I stopped, took a breath, and tried for true politeness. 'That's kind of short notice, but if she has something special she has to do, maybe we could still change the date.'

Renee frowned at the amplifier. 'Do you have a safety pin?'

Well, what could I say? I went to the all-purpose drawer, found one, and gave it to her. She didn't even say thanks.

'Renee,' I said, 'how come when I make a perfectly reasonable suggestion you always act like I'm stupid or something?'

'You're not stupid.'

She opened the safety pin and poked gently at a wire, twiddled a dial or two, plugged everything in, and struck a chord.

'There,' she said to no one in particular. Then she unplugged everything and started packing up. 'We might as well get this upstairs,' she said, apparently to me. 'It'll save time when Steve gets back.'

Renee's touchy about her equipment; she doesn't like anyone else to handle it, so this was a compliment – two, if you counted 'not stupid'. On the last trip I took up a speaker, with two Cokes cradled under my arm. We set everything down gently and sat down on the front steps to wait for Steve.

I opened my Coke. 'So if I'm not stupid, then what's "or something"?'

Renee opened her Coke and sighed.

'My mother's always busy-and-can't-make-it so I don't have to ask her, OK?'

'OK,' I said. I'd known Renee since we were in first grade, just like I'd known the others, even Jan, although she was in Catholic school until seventh, but all I really knew about Renee's mother was how she looked.

'Renee,' I said, 'that's still not – what am I supposed to know about your mom without you telling me?'

Renee thought about that for a minute.

'You're right. It's stupid to think that everybody knows they wanted a boy. My dad did, anyway. My mother didn't want anything.'

'Anything?'

'Any children. I heard them once. She said, "Charles, I refuse to try again. Renee ruined my figure as it is. I absolutely refuse."'

'Ruined her figure?' I interrupted without thinking. 'Gorgeous Georgia Austin?'

Renee drank some more of her Coke.

'Her name is Louise.'

'I know, I mean I didn't know it was Louise, but my mom just calls her that sometimes. You know, my parents and yours go to some of the same parties. And if my father's had three drinks instead of two, he tends to mention how beautiful she is.'

I was babbling, saying the wrong thing. I kept going, trying for the right one.

'Anyway, last time that happened my mom said that Gorgeous Georgia wasn't the only looker in the family, she said your father is very –' Oh Tammy you jerk, I thought, when will you learn to quit while you're behind – 'attractive,' I finished lamely.

'Yeah.' Renee looked straight ahead of her, with kind of a half-smile. 'I guess I'm the only one in my family who isn't.'

'But –' I shut my mouth. *Think* before you speak.

While I was thinking, Renee's eyebrows went up in a way I've learned not to like.

'Well?' she said.

'Well, at least you're not fat,' I offered.

She just kind of snorted.

'And you're not – you're not really ugly.'

'Flattery will get you nowhere.'

'Renee, *please* don't turn sarcastic on me,' I begged. 'Anyway, I didn't know you cared. You never act like it.'

'I suppose you mean', she said with her most infuriating sneer, 'that I don't cut out and save all those tips in *Seventeen* magazine about How to Make the Best of Your Looks.'

'Or those little pointers on How to Make the Most of Your Personality,' I snapped back.

Renee looked at me with a surprised expression. Then she laughed – not sneered, laughed. She licked her finger and drew an up-and-down line in the air. That means 'score one for you'. Those points are hard to come by, and from Renee of all people! I was flattered, but Renee was looking down at the steps again.

'Tammy, it isn't not being beautiful like her –'

'Who could be?' I said.

And it's true. Renee's mom isn't the kind just men look at; I had to look twice the first time I met her, in third grade, just to be sure I really was in the same room with someone that beautiful. She probably glows in the dark.

Renee didn't look up.

'Tammy, if I were even as pretty as you are.'

She sounded so sad that I couldn't feel offended, and I wouldn't have anyway. I'm no Caroline, but I like the way I look, and if I ever need to look better I can always start saving those hints from *Seventeen*.

'But why?' I asked. 'Nobody dates that much in eighth grade. Maybe some, but it's not like you have to sit around feeling like a creep if you're not busy on Saturday night.'

She looked at me for a second, but she didn't say anything.

She was making me think, which is bad enough from a teacher and really mean from a friend, but she probably didn't mean it.

'OK,' I said, 'I know that how popular you are depends on what you look like, but not that much, unless it's really extreme one way or the other; and you're not that bad off. I mean, not so that anybody minds.'

Renee swallowed so hard that I heard it.

'Suppose it made a difference with your parents?'

'What?' was all I could manage.

Renee didn't say anything. I thought about some of my friends' mothers. My favourite is Jan's. She can't remember my name, but she always remembers me. Have you ever noticed that sometimes even when you don't like a kid that much you really like her mother? Not Renee's. There wasn't that much to like or dislike, I hardly ever saw her, but when I did she didn't see me. She just said whatever she thought she was supposed to say and looked right through me. She was kind of a zero, except for the way she looked.

'When I was ten,' Renee said, 'she was going to get me plastic surgery for my nose.'

That stopped me cold. Renee's nose isn't ten feet

long or anything, it's not even a Barbra Streisand nose. It's just a nose. Like her father's, I noticed the next time I saw him. Maybe it would look better on a boy, but plastic surgery? On a little girl?

'My father said no, absolutely not. Since then I guess she's just kind of lost interest.'

But at least somebody was on her side, I thought.

'What about your father?'

'He's OK. But I'm not a boy or even a pretty girl, and anyway I'm a kid so I'm Her department. Besides, he's not home that much.'

'Yeah,' I said, because it figured. I saw his name once in *Time* magazine, so I knew that he wasn't just a neurosurgeon, he was an eminent neurosurgeon. *Time* said so.

The sound of the horn made us both jump. We hadn't even noticed the van pulling up in front of the house.

While we were picking up the stuff to take it out to the van, I said:

'Since they can't come to the barbecue, then you'll tell them yourself about the group?'

'If they ask.'

'*Renee* –!'

She gave me a funny look. It was amused, concerned, and something else I couldn't put my finger on.

'Honestly, Tam,' she said, 'it's not that they don't care about me. They just aren't that interested, OK?'

It was beef stew for dinner that night. I volunteered to peel the potatoes, a job Mom and I both hate. It must be hereditary. Sitting in the good-smelling kitchen, trying not to notice the slimy potato peelings, I glanced over every once in a while at my mother, peeling carrots, making salad; I thought about Gorgeous Georgia Austin, and shivered. When I'd finished and dropped the peels in the garbage disposal she said, 'Thank you, love.'

'You're welcome,' I said. 'Mom?'

I thought I saw a faint grin, but she didn't look up from the cake she was icing. 'What is it?'

'I know how you feel about doing your own inviting to the barbecue, but I want you to ask Renee's dad, Dr Austin. You should probably call him at his office, he's not home that much. You could – just tell him it's important.'

I fidgeted, looked around for something to do, started to get the plates down from the cupboard. Mom put the potatoes into the stew.

'Are you sure it's necessary?'

'No,' I admitted. 'In fact, I'm not even sure if it's a good idea. But the thing is, I've only met him once or twice, and you know him and I thought –'

'OK.'

'Will you do it tomorrow?'

The grown-up to grown-up feeling vanished.

'Tammy,' she said, 'I know when the barbecue is. We're giving it, remember?'

Friday morning at school, Renee stopped me in the hall on the way to English – supposedly to ask me about something, really to mention casually that her father was coming to the barbecue.

'He's cancelling a conference.' She sounded awed.

Renee, of all people. 'A conference. In Milwaukee. He said he thought the Neurological Association could get along without him for once.'

'Oh.'

'Anyway,' she stopped and took a breath. 'Thanks.'

14

Friday evening finally came. I was in charge of stuffing celery and answering the door. They all looked a little puzzled when they walked in – all the parents, that is. Jan, Monica, and Caroline just looked nervous. By the time I opened the door for Renee and her father I felt like saying, 'No doubt you're wondering why I called you all here tonight,' but they both looked cool as cucumbers.

Renee said, 'Tammy, have you met my father?' He smiled and said, 'I'm not sure,' and we shook hands. For someone that old, he is pretty attractive.

Parents safely steered out to the patio, the Tigers began drifting into the kitchen.

'When?' Jan said when she came inside.

'When what?'

'Listen, Tammy,' Caroline said, 'this better be good.'

'Don't worry,' I said. 'My mom makes the best barbecue in –'

'Don't give me that,' Caroline said.

'Manners! Anyway, what's everyone so nervous about?'

'We're not that nervous,' Monica said. 'They are. The parents.'

'Yeah,' I said. 'I noticed.'

'Well, us too,' Jan said.

'Speak for yourself,' I told her.

'Oh no, Tammy dear.' Caroline spoke very politely. 'That's your job, remember?'

I stepped back from the table to keep a drop of sweat from falling onto the celery.

'Tammy' – Jan sounded anxious – 'you have figured out what you're going to say, haven't you?'

'I DON'T –' I stopped and calmly started over again. 'I don't know why everyone's making such a big deal about this.'

Caroline rolled her eyes. I glared at her. As a matter of fact, I'd been counting on a burst of inspiration at the last minute, but the last minute seemed to be just around the corner and so far, no inspiration.

Renee came in from the patio.

'So this is where everybody is. We're all supposed to be passing around hors d'oeuvres and I'm the only one who's doing it.'

She picked up the tray of stuffed celery.

'Tammy, your mom said to tell you that she's ready to start the steaks. I think you'd better tell them now, before they're all too busy eating.'

I took the tray of celery out of her hands and set it back on the table.

'OK, I will. Right now. And the rest of you can hide in here, or you can come with me.'

I thought our mass entrance onto the patio would make more of an impression than it did. Of course, the kitchen door just leads onto the corner of it. The parents were gathered in around the barbecue in a sort of semicircle. Dad was tending bar, Mom was brushing barbecue sauce on the steaks and hostessing away. Nobody even looked at us.

I thought of an opening line, gave an unbelievably idiotic little giggle, and said: 'I guess you're all wondering why I called you here tonight.'

My voice cracked. How interesting, just like a boy's. But it didn't matter, because no one heard me except the other Tigers.

'Some leader,' Renee said. She didn't even bother to sneer.

That did it. After all I'd done for her, and I'd actually begun to feel that we were really friends! I shot her one hate-filled glance, whirled around and yelled:

'HEY YOU GUYS!'

It got their attention.

'I have something to tell you,' I went on in a more reasonable voice, 'about the group.' Without looking back to see what the others were doing, I walked to stand in front of the barbecue.

'What I – what we – want to tell you about is this. We're not professionals or anything, but we've worked hard to get as good as we are.'

They were looking surprised, dubious, impressed – anyway, I definitely had their attention.

'We're good enough to get any kind of a job that groups our age are hired to play for, but for a long time we didn't get any because kids would rather hear boy musicians.'

I paused to let that sink in and to think what to say next.

Caroline's mother almost did it for me.

'I know. I've told Caroline how very proud I am of all of you. You must be very good indeed to overcome that handicap.'

She glanced over her shoulder at Caroline who, with the others, had edged up to the fringes of the group.

Caroline cleared her throat and looked at me.

'As a matter of fact,' I said, 'we're not. I mean we haven't. What I mean is, the name of our group is Tommy and the Tigers, and as far as the kids we play for and the people who hire us know, we're boys!'

They took it pretty well. Caroline's father laughed so hard he almost fell off his chair, and the others thought it was pretty funny too, except for Monica's father. He doesn't have much sense of humour – Monica says it's not his fault; corporation lawyers never do. But he was the parent we'd been the most worried about.

While the others were being surprised and laughing and asking questions, he just sat there looking expressionless, but he didn't shout or faint or anything, so I guess he more or less accepted it after a while.

Jan's father buried his face in his hands, but you could still hear him loud and clear. 'Four boys,' he said, 'and at last a girl and her the sweetest little thing God ever made, and she wants to be a –'

I didn't get to hear the rest, because Monica's father had started to laugh. I'd never seen him so much as smile before.

Caroline's mother was being kind of quiet – for her, anyway. She looked puzzled, as though she were trying to figure out whether we were being liberated or unliberated. That made me wonder about it myself, so I went and asked her.

I didn't really care very much which it was, but I was curious, and anyway I wanted to butter her up a little.

Caroline's mother is not my favourite person in the world, but she is a good one to have on your side.

'Well,' she said, 'I guess it's a little of both.'

Some answer. I decided to think that over when I had the time.

15

It was exciting when the posters for the Midsummer Fling started to appear, even if they didn't mention the name of our group. They just said 'Live Rock Music, 2–6 P.M.'

We got some tiger-print cotton, and our mothers helped us work out outfits that weren't as hot as the others but still looked boyish. And we made a big banner with our name on it out of black and gold felt to hang over the bandstand.

Steve worked out the hook-up with the Recreation Department. They had loudspeakers in the trees, and it sounded just great; I mean it was really loud.

Caroline bought a pair of dark glasses with enormous lenses. They looked so good we all decided to get some. As Caroline pointed out, how often do you get to combine glamour with safety? Then we were all ready to go, with our outfits on and our hair smoothed out (or our wig on) and our dark glasses. My mother checked us over.

'Well,' she said. 'I'm not saying your own mothers wouldn't recognize you . . .'

'But you don't think anyone else would, right, Mom?' I asked.

'Right,' said my mother. 'Good luck, son.'

She thought that was pretty funny.

Anyway, there was one person who knew exactly what 'Live Rock Music' meant, and she was waiting for us when we got there. A lot of kids were hanging around, and more of them drifted over towards the stand when we started setting up, but Didi was waiting for *us*.

'Eeeek!' she shrieked. 'There they are! And there's Ronnie!' She had her friends with her: I recognized them from the party.

Kids are just like anyone else. If someone says 'Eeeek, there they are!' other kids will think that 'they' must be something special.

'Who's that?' someone asked Didi, as Steve and Renee were putting up our banner.

'Tommy and the Tigers,' she said. 'But the really cute one is Ron, that tall boy over there.'

'Oh yeah?' said this really interested voice. Fortunately, I had my back turned. All this was going on about two feet from the stand, and I didn't have to turn around to realize that Scott Bailey was there. In fact, I didn't plan to turn around at all.

By the time we were ready to start and I had to turn around, there was enough of a crowd so that he'd been pushed away from the stand – at least I couldn't spot him.

I did see a lot of other kids I knew. But once we started playing it was easy to relax and figure, well, they'll recognize us or they won't, and there's nothing we can do about it now.

Anyway, they didn't; and it wasn't just the costumes and dark glasses and stuff, although that helped, of course. It was because I'd been right (the Born Leader has no false modesty). They were looking at five boys, so they were seeing five boys. We all noticed the same expression on some of their faces – an expression that

77

said 'Where have I seen that kid before?' But since they were wondering where they'd seen that *boy* before, they never recognized us.

It was great. We sounded really good and really loud, and the kids loved it. We had to play 'Didi Darling' twice.

As usual, we didn't have any trouble at all while we were playing. Just once, while stone-face Renee (or Ronnie) was doing her guitar solo, and Didi and her crowd of fans were gazing up adoringly, she let them have a slight sneer. They went wild.

Mostly, though, everyone danced and we played and things were fine. But afterward, when we were packing up, all these stupid girls kept milling around, and then all of a sudden there was a reporter.

I guess he was assigned to cover the Midsummer Fling for our local paper, and since nothing special was happening, he decided that we were news because we were kids. That is one reason our local paper is so boring; nothing much ever happens around here, but they think they have to print something anyway.

He wanted to know how long we'd been playing together, where else we'd played, and how we'd gotten started.

'Well,' I said, 'a bunch of us fellows just sort of got together.' What had I been worried about? He wasn't going to ask what sex we were, after all.

No. He just wanted to know our names.

'I'm Tommy,' I said, 'and this is Ron and George and Jimmy and Sebastian.'

'Sebastian Fox,' said Monica.

I could have kicked her. I'd been hoping that if none

of us gave last names, he'd forget to ask or something. We could make some up, of course, but I didn't want to do that if we could help it.

But he was fairly old, about twenty-eight or so, and I guess he wasn't sure what the tribal customs were among kids our age; anyway, he hesitated for a minute and then asked what school we went to.

A hiccup from Jan. All of us were thinking the same thing. There are only two junior high schools around here, not counting Roosevelt, and they're not very big. All the kids at Adams or Swanson more or less know each other, and someone must read that stupid paper. Everyone takes it, for some reason. All I could think of was this poem I learned when I was little that went 'Oh what a tangled web we weave, when first we practise to deceive,' which was very true but no help at all.

The silence must have lasted only about thirty seconds when we were saved – not by the bell, but by a screeching of brakes, a crunch, and the sound of breaking glass. Two cars had just run into each other in the intersection at the corner of the park.

Our reporter ran off to investigate. I have to tell you right now that no one was killed or anything. I called the police the next morning to make sure, because it's terrible to be so glad that someone has had an accident.

But if the mayor's troubles were just beginning (it turned out that he was driving one of the cars and had run a red light – for once our local paper had something to print), ours were not exactly over.

We had gotten our equipment and our nerve-racked selves into the van and were on the way home, when

Renee looked out the back window and said, 'There's a car following us.'

'So?' I said.

'It's got Didi in it,' she said.

Yes, it was Didi, dear determined Didi. She wasn't actually driving the car, of course, but whoever was driving definitely wasn't her mother. They were following their darling Ronnie home to see where he lived, just like real groupies. Steve did everything he could to lose them, but it was no use. We finally had to let Renee out fifteen blocks from her house, wearing Monica's Michael Jackson wig. She didn't even complain; all she said, as she crouched by the door ready for Steve to slow down and let her out, was 'Are you sure Mick Jagger started like this?'

Now that's what I call taking it like a real pro. Especially compared to Monica, who carried on like she was lending out a mink coat. Not that it was that easy on the rest of us, even if Steve did manage to shake them long enough for us to run into the emergency entrance of Our Lady of Mercy Hospital and out through the lobby. As Caroline would say, that's showbiz.

The one I was really worried about was Scott. Sure enough, he stopped me the next day as we were leaving the classroom. He looked really angry.

'I saw Tommy and the Tigers yesterday,' he said.

'Oh?' I said politely. 'I didn't see you.'

'I didn't see you, either,' he said.

'How do you think they sound?' I asked. For some reason I really wanted to know.

'You know darn well how they sound.'

My stomach froze.

'They sang "Didi Darling",' he said. 'That's your song; you wrote it. I heard you do it, only with different words and a different tempo.'

'Well, uh, they sort of changed it,' I croaked.

'You bet they changed it, sweetheart. It sounds about ten times better. And they sound about ten times better than your stupid all-girl band ever could.'

'Oh, yes!' I breathed. I was too relieved to pretend any better than that.

Scott stared at me.

'So why did you give them all your arrangements?'

'Well, uh . . .' I stammered. 'We, uh, we were dis-banding anyway, and we –'

'And just to get even with me you not only gave them all your stuff, you tricked me into losing that job to them.'

I fixed my eyes on the floor and hoped I was looking guilty.

'Gee, Scott,' I said. 'I'm sorry.'

Then Scott got this very superior expression on his face.

'You know, Tammy,' he said, 'I used to think you were different from other girls.'

I could only turn and flee down the hall. When I sneaked a peek back around the corner, he was stand-ing just where I had left him, looking puzzled.

16

I met Monica outside in front of the school – we were going downtown to buy new strings for her electric bass.

As we were heading for the bus stop, and I was starting to tell Monica all about Genius Bailey and his wonderful theory, we were stopped by a boy neither of us had ever seen before. He was black; he looked about fifteen, and like he might be on a football team.

'Hey,' he said. 'Either of you girls know a guy called Sebastian Fox?'

We both answered at once.

'No,' I said.

'Yes,' said Monica.

'I think I've seen him around. Maybe,' I added hastily.

The boy looked around toward the school.

'Swanson, huh? I thought so,' he said, more to himself than to us. Then he turned back to us.

'Well, the next time you see him around, maybe, you can tell him this from me. I don't want my girl carrying around any pictures of Sebastian Fox, or writing any letters to Sebastian Fox, or seeing Sebastian Fox.'

I was too paralysed to get my mouth open.

'We'll tell him,' said Monica.

'Good,' said the boy. Then he turned around and headed back toward the bus stop.

Monica and I made two decisions on the spot: 1. The next rehearsal would be combined with a business meeting, including Steve. We knew he had to be at the bottom of this. 2. We would take a later bus.

We were right about Steve. Next Saturday afternoon he explained to five unsympathetic listeners what he'd been up to.

'After that Midsummer Fling you girls got some fan mail. And I figured it would be good publicity to answer it. I mean, if you're going to be a success at this, you can use some fans. And I'd like to see you make some real money. As it is, my twenty per cent barely covers the gas for the van.'

'Tisk, tisk,' said Caroline.

'It started with that picture from Didi's party,' said Steve. 'She wanted Ron to autograph it for her, and since I figured you might not want to –'

'You bet I wouldn't,' said Renee grimly.

'– because someone might recognize your hand-writing,' he swept on smoothly, 'I did it myself and mailed it back to her. Then these letters came, saying how much kids liked the group, so I got some prints made of the pictures I took at the Midsummer Fling and autographed them for you.

'Mostly I just put "Best Wishes, Tommy and the Tigers", but a couple more of the letters were to Renee, and a couple were for you, Tammy, and one was for Monica/Sebastian.'

'We figured out that much,' said Monica.

'None for you or Jan, so far,' he told Caroline, 'but don't give up hope.'

'I'll cry myself to sleep,' said Caroline.

We finally agreed that if we got any more fan mail, we would answer it ourselves, but no more pictures.

It was much too late.

The next afternoon the phone rang and I answered it on the upstairs extension.

'Hi, there,' said a voice. 'This is Scott.'

'What did you call for?' I asked.

'I'm coming over to discuss something with you,' he said.

'I won't be here.'

He said, 'Yes, you will, Tommy.'

I was still standing with the receiver in my hand, staring at the wall, when he rang the front doorbell.

17

I put the phone down and answered the door. Neither of us said anything as he followed me down to the rumpus room. I closed the door, turned around to face him, and said, 'How?'

He handed me the manila envelope he was carrying. Inside was an enlargement of the picture Didi had had taken at her party – the one of her and Renee.

It was Renee, all right. You could tell at a glance. Here is something to remember if you are going to disguise yourself: a picture can be easier to recognize than an actual person. Anyway, when I saw it, it made sense that Scott had been able to stand twenty feet away from Renee for a whole afternoon and not recognize her and then had spotted her right away in the picture. I turned it over. On the back Steve had written, 'Best of luck to a Real Cute Girl, from Ronnie.' It could have been worse, but I still hoped that Renee never saw it.

I handed the photo back to him. 'Where?' I said.

'This friend of mine took me to Didi's house yesterday,' he said. 'We were playing records, and she was raving about Tommy and the Tigers, and she showed it to us.'

'How did you get her to give it to you?' I asked.

'I told her I knew someone who knew a record producer who might give Ronnie his big break,' Scott said, looking pleased with himself. He was feeling really proud of having thought up that big fat lie so he

85

could get hold of this poor little nerd's most cherished possession. And this person had me in his power. No, he had all of us in his power, thanks to me.

'What are you going to do?' I asked, to make conversation while I decided on the best way to kill myself.

Scott said, 'I'll tell you what I'm going to do if you'll quit staring at the wall like that. You're making me nervous.'

I stared at Scott. He did look nervous. I'd seen and read plenty of stories where the evil beast has the heroine in his clutches, but I'd never seen the E.B. look nervous about it.

'Well?' I said.

'I won't tell anyone, if I can join the group.'

I looked at him and I knew he meant it. He was still nervous, but he was dead serious. He reminded me vaguely of someone, but I couldn't think who. I realized that killing myself was a childish fantasy. The thing to do was to convince my family to move to Australia, change our last name, and start a new life. But we probably couldn't get all that done in one day. I needed time.

'I need time,' I said aloud.

'Time for what, to think of a way out? Don't bother, there isn't one.'

'I guess that means if we don't let you join, you'll tell.'

He nodded.

'But why?' I asked reasonably. 'You said we sounded dumb, and who wanted to work with a bunch of girls, and –'

'Tammy,' he interrupted, 'look at the wall again because I don't like the way you're looking at me, but listen. I never said nobody wanted to work with a bunch of girls, I said nobody wanted to listen to a bunch of girls. And I was right, or you wouldn't be pretending you were boys. That was pretty clever, by the way. Whose idea was it?'

'Mine,' I said modestly.

'Thought so. Just wanted to make sure you were paying attention.'

'Why don't we continue this conversation on top of a tall building?' I suggested.

He went on as though I hadn't spoken.

'I always used to put your group down because I was jealous. I couldn't get the guys in my group to practise the way you did. We always ended up playing records and jamming and horsing around, and besides you had Renee, so you sounded better than we did.'

Much better. But flattery does not work on the Born Leader. 'What about your group?' I asked. 'Are we supposed to adopt all of you, like the Brady Bunch?'

'We disbanded,' he said. 'Anyway, I told them last week I was quitting. They can go on if they want to.'

'But Scott,' I pleaded, 'you can't organize a group and then leave like that. You owe them some loyalty. Walking out on them is mean and selfish and —'

'At least it's not sneaky,' said Scott.

'Uh, no,' I mumbled, 'not sneaky exactly.'

'Like the way you got that job in the park, the one I told you about.'

'Exactly,' I cried. 'Who would want to work with such sneaky, rotten girls?'

Scott gave me his famous smile. 'As a matter of fact,' he said, 'I'm pretty low-down myself.'

'No kidding,' I said, without smiling back.

'Well,' he said, 'I'll just give you a day or so to break the news to the rest of the guys. Let me know when the next rehearsal is.' Then he left.

18

I didn't tell the others over the phone; I just told them to be prepared for a shock. But I was the one who had a shock coming.

When I told them about Scott finding out and wanting to join the group, nobody said anything for a minute. Then Renee said, 'Playing what?'

This unspeakable thing had happened, and all she cared about was whether she'd still be lead guitar. Needless to say, I hadn't even thought about it.

'He didn't say. Back-up guitar and vocals, maybe.'

'All right, I guess.' Monica sighed. 'But if we had to take in somebody else, we really could have used an electric keyboard.'

Ever since I'd talked to Scott, I'd been racking my brain to find a way to keep them from killing me, and now I was spluttering: 'But how can you be so calm about this – this *boy*, and Scott Bailey of all people, horning in on our group?'

'It's supposed to be a boys' group, isn't it?' said Caroline.

Who can fight that kind of logic?

'And why "of all people"?' asked Monica. 'At least he can hold a beat and carry a tune; he's the only one of those turkeys he played with who could.'

'You don't understand how hard this is for Tammy,' Jan said earnestly. 'She can't stand Scott.'

'Then isn't it too bad that Tammy's the one who got us into this?' said Caroline, not very nicely.

'Anyway,' Monica said, 'he may think he's God's gift to girls, but he doesn't act that awful most of the time. Just when he's around you.'

'That doesn't make any sense. Why would he just be that way around me?'

They all looked at each other.

'Well maybe,' Jan said in her brave little mouse way, 'maybe, Tammy, it's because you always act so awful around him.'

This was too hideous to be true. 'Are you telling me,' I said, slowly and distinctly, 'that not only do you agree to have him in the Tigers, but I'm supposed to be nice to him?'

'Would you rather have him spread it all over town who we really are?' said Caroline.

The Born Leader knows when she is licked.

'It's not going to be easy,' I said.

'In that case,' said Renee, 'you'll just have to make the most of your personality, won't you?'

I met her eyes and suddenly remembered that crack I'd made about the pointers in *Seventeen*.

'Touché,' I said.

'Does Steve know?' Caroline asked.

'Yeah, I told him. In fact he's bringing Scott here this afternoon.'

We'd just finished setting up when Steve came charging down the stairs into the basement, with Scott in tow.

'Guess what, girls,' he said, 'Scott here talked his mother into getting him an electric piano!'

Monica beamed. 'Hey, that's great!'

'It's just a used one,' Scott said. So big deal; all our equipment was, except for Renee's. 'To get it I had to promise to start regular piano lessons again. She only let me quit last year.'

Four of us looked impressed by this sacrifice.

He gave us all this shy, humble look he must have practised in front of a mirror and said, 'It's really OK, then, I can join?'

I felt like throwing up. The rest of them fell for it, so far as I could see, so what would be the point of their so-called leader announcing the decision?

'There's just one thing,' Renee said, almost casually.

'As long as you don't tell,' said Monica.

'Because if you do,' said Caroline, 'we'll spread so many stories about you that no girl at Swanson will ever go out with you again.'

Then Jan spoke up. 'And if you go on to North High with us,' she said, looking so sweet and sincere, like an angel ready to take off for heaven, 'we'll make sure that no girl there will ever go out with you, either.' You could tell that she meant it.

Scott looked scared for a minute. Who wouldn't? Then he grinned.

'Why should I tell? It's my group too, now. And I'm looking forward to playing with you. You guys are dynamite.'

'We know,' said Renee.

After another second of silence – just long enough for Scott's grin to get a little uncertain around the edges – Monica grinned back and stuck out her hand. 'You're in,' she said. 'Sebastian's the name. Sebastian Fox.'

Then all of a sudden it was happy hour; smiles, handshakes, which I managed to avoid, and everybody piling upstairs to help unload Scott's piano, leaving me alone to brood for a minute.

Where had those stony-faced amazons been when I needed them? They'd almost scared me, and out of the corner of my eye I could see even Steve looking nervous. With an act like that we probably could have frightened Scott off without having to take him into the group at all. We could have tried, anyway. We? Who was I kidding? Where had the leader been during this whole discussion – nowhere, that's where. Maybe I should just drop out; who needed me anyway? They could rename the group, call it Scott and the Snakes in the Grass.

There was just one problem with that. We got the piano set up and started playing, some fooling around, some numbers, Scott getting used to us and us getting used to the piano. He caught on fast, and he'd already learned a lot of our material. The fact was that it sounded very good. He really added to the group – musically that is.

It was so exciting we didn't want to quit at five, so everybody called home and we had hot dogs and Cokes right there, and went on until nine. We were sounding so good I almost forgot that I hated Scott Bailey's guts.

Afterward, when they were all patting each other on the back and saying how glad they were he'd joined the group, I remembered. I started clearing up the paper plates and leftovers. Scott followed me over to the counter where I was collecting the trash to take up-stairs.

'Can I help?'

I closed my eyes for a second. I would do what Renee said and make the most of a rotten situation.

'The Coke bottles go in that crate in the corner.'

'OK,' he said. But he didn't move. 'Tammy, I know you're mad because of how I got into the group, and maybe you have a right to be. But now that I'm in, and I've shown that I can keep up with the rest of you –'

I was keeping my eyes on my work, scraping left-overs off the paper plates and putting them in the trash, but I glanced around at him.

He was looking shy and embarrassed. I didn't say anything; just kept scraping plates.

'What I mean is – well – while we're working together, couldn't we be . . . friends?'

What an act. If I didn't know better I would have thought he meant it, and so what if he did? How could I explain to anyone, let alone to him, that this was supposed to be *my* group. How could it be now?

I put the last plate into the trash and turned to look him in the eye.

'Scott,' I said, 'there are only two things that matter. One is how good a musician you are, and you're as good as I am, which means you're as good as any of us. Except Renee, of course. The other one is how it affects the morale of the rest of the group to be working with a blackmailer. If they don't mind,' it was hard to hold my voice steady, 'I don't.'

Just for a second he looked at me like I'd slapped him, then he smiled (sort of).

'OK,' he said, 'if that's the way you want it.'

He didn't say anything else, just turned around and walked back to the others. But the look he gave me made me feel so bad, I had to remind myself that it was just an act.

19

Contrary to my hopes, Scott was never late for rehearsals. And either he was a fast learner or he practised a lot, because he got the arrangements down fast. He was the most conscientious of all of us, too, about rehearsing our numbers and not just having jam sessions, even though he and Renee tried out some really wild stuff when they were just fooling around. One number they worked out sounded almost like jazz. Renee wanted to play it at our next job.

'No,' I said.

'Why not?' said Monica. 'I like it.'

'Because they won't dance to it,' said Caroline.

'Well, I'm tired of this stupid kid stuff,' snarled Renee.

I opened my mouth to tell her what I thought of that, but Scott got in first.

'Renee,' he said gently, 'that's who we're playing for. Kids.'

He could have pointed out that we were kids ourselves, but that wasn't really the point. Renee was our age, but when it came to music she was more like a grown-up. Although she certainly wasn't acting like a grown-up.

No one was. We had three homecoming dances coming up that September, and what with those and rehearsing and school starting (and we had to keep our grades up, too, so our parents would let us go on with the group), everyone's temper was getting ragged. I guess Scott was on his good behaviour or something, because he did calm things down more than once.

I should also explain about our sound. That's what Renee referred to as 'stupid kid stuff'. The kids didn't just like us because they thought we were boys – they liked the kind of music we played. We did mostly golden oldies from the late fifties and early sixties. They liked to dance to them. I was the one who decided we should do that kind of music. I told the others it would be popular, and it was, so I was proud of that. It showed that I was a Born Leader. Anyway, I like those songs myself; I was about to tell Renee to go to New York, if she wanted, and take heroin and be a big shot jazz musician, when Scott intervened. The group just wasn't what it used to be.

Didi showed up at all three dances. I think that Steve kept her posted on where we'd be playing so she could be there and scream 'Ronnie!' and impress everyone with how well known we were.

It did sort of work that way. She would usually bring friends, and the kids already there would be impressed that we had fans. But we all had enough sense not to point out the positive side of Didi and her banshees when Renee was around. She was beginning to get a hunted look, disappearing like a flash when we took a break, and when the dance was over, she would refuse to come out and take down her equipment until the last kid had gone. Even then, I think she expected to find Didi hiding behind an amplifier. We couldn't blame her.

To tell the truth, Scott was helpful about that, too. He would head them off at the pass and talk to Didi. She was pathetically grateful, since he was the only member of the group who would. He could use his real name and his real school and his real sex and everything, so it was easier for him.

Going home in the van after the third dance, Renee asked about Scott and Didi. 'Maybe next time the Nerd will be yelling "Scottie!"' she suggested hopefully.

'I wouldn't mind,' said Scott. 'She is kind of cute.' There's no accounting for tastes. 'But all we ever talk about is what Ronnie has for breakfast and what's Ronnie's favourite colour and . . .'

'And her idol is sulking behind the scenes,' said Caroline. 'Arrogant, that's what they call it in the fan magazines. "Has success spoiled Ronnie?"'

Caroline had gone too far, and we all knew it. Steve quickly changed the subject.

'Scott has a great idea about our name,' he said.

'What's wrong with our name?' I asked.

'Nothing, but he suggested that we should spell *tigers* with a *y*.'

I thought it over. Tommy and the Tygers. Kind of a nifty idea. Too bad it was Scott's.

Of course, I said it was a silly idea, and Jan sided with me because she is very loyal. Caroline didn't like it because she has no imagination about some things, and *tigers* is spelled with an *i*.

Monica liked the idea; Scott liked it, of course; and Renee sided with them, probably out of spite.

Steve said he would break the tie.

I said that I should be the one to break the tie. Since I was the leader, I should have two votes.

'Gee, I don't know, Tammy,' said Renee. 'Let's vote on that.'

Everybody laughed except me, and after that we were Tommy and the Tygers. In a way I was glad, because I liked the new name better. But it used to be my group.

That Thursday, Scott called me after school and said that he wanted to have a business meeting after next Saturday's rehearsal and that Steve should be there. He wouldn't tell me or anyone else what it was about. I figured that this had better be worth it, because if he was just throwing his weight around, then Tommy and the Tygers wasn't big enough for both of us.

We were all so curious that we decided to hold the business meeting first. Everyone, Steve included, was there at one o'clock sharp.

'OK, Scott,' I said. 'What is it?'

'The Play-off,' he said.

The Play-off had started as a contest for all the high-school bands in the state. The best ones each year would get to play in the big parade at the state capital, where they hold the finale. Then it had expanded to include junior-high groups, too. And the last couple of years there had been a special category for jazz and rock groups.

The Play-off was a pretty big deal. The winners got to be on a local TV show in the capital, and the year before last the winning rock group even cut a record. It wasn't exactly a hit, except maybe in their home-town, and nobody ever heard of them again, but they were pretty famous around here for a week or two.

Finally Caroline said, 'What about the Play-off?'

'The principal stopped me in the hall last Thursday and asked me to come and see him in his office after school. It turned out he wanted to ask about Tommy and the Tygers. He's heard of us. Then he wanted to know if any of the other Tygers went to Swanson.'

'What did you say?' whispered Jan.

'I said I didn't think so. I know it was a stupid answer, but I couldn't think of anything else to say. I didn't even know why he wanted to know.'

Even I had to nod agreement. We knew what it was like fending off questions like that from other kids, let alone from the principal.

Scott went on. 'He looked at me kind of funny and said that was a shame, because this year they were thinking of entering a popular music combo (that's what he called it) in the Play-off as well as the school band, only of course the members should all be students at Swanson.'

I was the only one who actually howled. The others just moaned.

'Then he said that if the other boys all went to schools in this district he could get in touch with the principals of their schools and work something out, especially if we made the finals. So I had to say mumble mumble, no thank you, sir.'

Total gloom. 'Is this why you called this meeting?' I said bitterly. 'So we could all know what we're missing?'

Jan spoke up. 'But we all go to Swanson,' she said.

'What good does that do?' said Monica.

'We'll just explain who we really are, and then we can go,' said Jan.

'NO!' said everybody else at once.

It wasn't that Jan wanted to go more than the rest of us did. She just wanted to stop pretending. I never could convince her that what we were doing was show business, not lying.

'Just a minute,' said Scott. 'I told you about it because I thought – we wouldn't tell everybody, but maybe if we explained –'

'To the principal?' Renee sneered and for once I couldn't blame her. 'About our "popular music combo"?'

But an idea was coming to the Born Leader.

'Miss Vincent!' I cried.

Everyone looked at me like I'd gone bananas, even Steve. He remembered her from when he went to Swanson.

'You're out of your mind,' he said flatly.

Miss Vincent is the vice-principal of our school. She looks like the Statue of Liberty, only she's a little taller and she's been there longer. She is sort of scary, but she's not mean. Whenever somebody gets caught smoking or cheating or anything else you can get suspended for, Miss Vincent is the one who does it. I had to go see her once for talking back to my English teacher. She is scary because of the way she looks you straight in the eye, but she isn't mean or unfair. I like her. Of course I'd never say anything like that around my friends, because it would make me sound like a freak.

That's exactly how they were looking at me.

'You actually expect the Wicked Witch of the West to help us out?' said Caroline.

'Well, I think if we explained . . .'

'We?' said Monica.

'All right, then, if *I* explained, she might understand. And even if she didn't, she might not tell on us.'

There was another silence, while everyone looked at the crazy person. Then Renee spoke.

'Tammy, if you really want to try this weirdo plan –'

'One of my weirdo plans worked, didn't it?' I interrupted hotly.

Renee continued as if I hadn't said anything, 'I might as well go with you.' I stared at her, wishing I could tell her how glad I was, how much better it would feel to have her with me.

'So will I, Tammy,' said Jan.

Her face told me exactly how she felt. She was terrified at the thought of facing Miss Vincent. But she is a good best friend. So I couldn't tell her, either, how I felt, which was that having her along would only make me more scared than I was already.

Maybe Monica understood. Anyway, she spoke up in that tone of voice she has when she's decided something.

'We'll all go.'

She looked sternly at Caroline, who said, 'Oh, well, all right.'

We all looked at Scott, who looked at the Beatles poster on the wall. Finally he said, 'It's different for you.'

'Why?' said Monica.

Scott looked at Steve, but he was no help. As far as Steve was concerned, the problem was solved, we'd won the Play-off, and he was arranging our personal appearance tour.

'She'll think it's funny. She'll laugh. I didn't even tell my own mother.'

'You mean you're embarrassed about working with a bunch of girls,' said Renee.

'That's the reason you only wanted to join the group after we'd changed,' said Caroline. 'This way no one knows you're working with girls.' She sounded really angry.

'Scott, are you in this group or not?' I said.

The strange thing is this: here was my perfect chance to show the others what a fake he really was, and for some reason, I wanted to be wrong.

Scott sighed. 'All right,' he said. 'We'll all go.'

20

I talked to Miss Vincent and made a special after-
school appointment. All we needed was for everybody
to see the six of us trooping into her office, and anyway
Steve had said he'd better come too – just so she'd
know we were on the level. Our parents said that
they'd back us up. (All the parents, that is, except
Scott's – he'd already told us that he didn't intend to
explain to them.) They'd back us up, but we had to talk
to her on our own. My father remembered Miss
Vincent from when Steve was at Swanson (he didn't
say why and neither did Steve), and he said he wouldn't
dare go to her with a story like that. Nothing like a
parent to give you self-confidence.

So we all went, and Guess Who was elected to tell
Miss Vincent our story. It's hard to talk to someone
who stares you straight in the eyes, especially if it's the
vice-principal and you're trying to make sense.

After I'd finished, she sat there and looked at us for
what seemed like half an hour. Then she pointed at
Scott.

'What are you doing here?' she said.

Whatever Scott had planned to say, it came out
sounding just like 'Urk'.

'He's a good musician,' I said quickly. 'And . . . and
we trust him.' The Born Leader knows when to put her
personal feelings aside. And it was true, more or less.
Anyway, Scott gave me such a grateful look that it was
true, at least right then.

I could tell that Miss Vincent knew there was more to it than that, but I think she's a Born Leader too. Anyway, she knows when it's time to drop the subject.

'Do your parents know about this?' she said.

We all nodded except Scott, who stared out of the window and said, 'My mother knows I belong to the group.'

She thought about it a little more. Then she said, 'You know, I've heard a lot of stories in this office, but this is the damned – I mean, the strangest one I've heard yet.'

Nobody had anything to say to that. We all listened to the quiet for another five minutes.

Finally she said, 'OK.'

Victory? 'But what about the principal?' I asked.

'Oh, I'll fix Revson,' she murmured absent-mindedly. Apparently she didn't notice the startled glances exchanged by those who were not Born Leaders.

Then she smiled at us. Nobody at school had ever seen her smile. It was a nice one, too.

'You know, Tammy,' she said, 'if I'd thought of that myself, I could have been a principal by now.'

Steve said, 'At least.'

I wasn't exactly sure what they were talking about, but I smiled back anyway. This time, even Renee would have to admit that, for once, I'd been right!

'There's just one thing, though,' said Miss Vincent. 'Since you're going to represent Swanson, and of course the school district, in the Play-off . . .'

It was great, the matter-of-fact way she said that. After all, everybody at Swanson knew that if Miss

Vincent said a thing was going to happen, it was going to happen.

'I think you'll have to give at least one performance here at your school.'

Everybody started talking at once, saying how we couldn't do it, we'd be recognized, etc.

Miss Vincent waited for the noise to die down. Then she said, 'How long do you plan to keep up this – this disguise?'

'Until after the Play-off,' said Jan. Jan? My best friend, the Mouse?

'Tammy says that they won't even give us a chance if they know we're girls,' she went on, 'and I guess she's right. But if we go to the Play-off and we do really well, if we win, then we're good enough to be ourselves and not have to fool anybody.'

I glared at Jan. 'You picked a fine time,' I began.

Miss Vincent interrupted. 'And if you don't . . . do well?'

'We will,' said Renee.

'But listen,' said Caroline, 'pretending we're boys at the Play-off will be easy' – famous last words – 'but here! The kids will know us.'

Miss Vincent smiled again, maybe not quite so nicely.

'I'm not worried about that,' she said. 'I'm sure that young people as ingenious as you seem to be will think of something. I think that the Halloween Hop will be just right.' Then she stood up and let us know that it was time to go.

21

Nobody congratulated me on the success of my brilliant idea.

'Wigs,' said Renee.

'Dark glasses,' said Monica.

'New outfits,' squeaked Jan. I think she was still very excited about the way she had put her foot down in Miss Vincent's office, but nobody said anything about that, either. I guess we all agreed without having to talk about it that the main thing was to get through the Halloween Hop, which was two weeks away.

'Where are we going to be?' said Caroline.

'Up on the stand, of course,' I said. 'You're not going to back out now, are you?'

'Back out?' said Caroline. Caroline usually sounds calm even when she isn't feeling that way, but her voice got a little shrill. 'Back *out*? And miss a chance to stand up in front of the whole school and pretend I'm a boy? No,' she said more calmly. 'I mean while George is playing in his group, where will Caroline be? I told Gary I'd go to the Hop with him.'

'Oooh,' said Jan. 'And I know Danny's going to ask me. We'll have to think of something. I mean, something that won't hurt his feelings,' she said anxiously.

As you may have noticed, Jan will never be a Born Leader. She has a genius for getting sidetracked.

'You could say yes and then be sick,' Scott suggested.

'That wouldn't be hard,' muttered Renee.

A flash! 'Just a minute,' I yelled. 'Masks! It's for Halloween, isn't it? We'll wear masks!'

'Oh, goody,' said Caroline, 'I'll be a Mickey Mouse and Jan can be a kitty-cat, and . . .'

'Not that kind, dummy,' I explained nicely. 'Eye masks, like the Lone Ranger's. No one will recognize us.'

Monica said that she never had any trouble recognizing the Lone Ranger, but everyone agreed it was a good idea.

'Do I have to wear a wig?' said Scott.

'Of course not,' I said. 'We want you to be recognized.'

'We do?' said Scott.

'Yes. They expect to see you there. We want them to see one boy they know and four boys they don't know.'

'Oh, I see,' said Scott. He sounded relieved. I wish I could have thought of a reason for making him wear a dress.

We called my mom in, because she and Monica were the best ones at clothes.

They got some black cotton material and made plain tops with a drawstring at the bottom. They were really tricky, because they were cut sort of full but they didn't look like it, especially from a distance. With our black jeans and tiger-striped waistcoats on, you didn't even notice the drawstring. We paid for the material with the money we'd made from the homecoming dances.

You should have seen us on Friday night. All the girls came to my house to get dressed. And everyone's mother came, except Renee's, but her father came.

We decided to put on our masks before we came downstairs; but first we looked at ourselves in the mirror. Not bad. We looked definitely scary and Halloweenish, but kind of neat at the same time, and so weird in our wigs and our black eye-masks with gold sequins around the edges.

We'd been saving the money from the homecoming dances for a set of tiger-striped drums for Caroline, but so much of that had gone for our wigs and the material for our clothes, that we decided to splurge on gold paint for our boots instead.

My wig was a sensible colour – about two shades darker than my own hair, and a nice smooth page-boy cut. Renee didn't need a wig. What she usually did for school was make some kind of pony tail with a rubber band and comb it once a week, at least that's what it looked like. But for the performance it was always shiny and fresh and brushed out neatly with a little curl at the ends.

We went downstairs. Our parents must have been pretty impressed, because no one said anything for a minute.

Finally Caroline's mother said, 'Caroline, is that you?'

My father said, 'I never thought I'd see my own daughter looking like something I'd be afraid to run into in a dark alley.'

I wanted them to be impressed, but not that impressed. So I yelled 'Arrrgh!' and jumped on him, landing in his lap. He said I'd scared the breath out of him, and we felt better.

Jan's mother looked at her uncertainly. 'You know,

Jan,' she said, 'I certainly would never allow you to wear a wig like that if you were — I mean if you weren't —'

'Well, I am,' said Jan. 'I mean, I'm not.'

'Don't worry, ma'am,' said Steve. 'I'll take care of her.' More famous last words.

Renee's father was staring at her. 'Renee,' he said, 'I always thought you looked too much like me to make a good-looking woman. Now I'm not so sure.'

I could sort of see what he meant. Pimples and all (and there were fewer of those lately), there was just something about her.

Renee turned away. She was actually blushing. I could tell that she didn't know what to say.

Jan squeaked anxiously. 'But she's not supposed to be a good-looking woman. She's supposed to be a good-looking boy!' and that made everybody laugh, and then Steve said, 'Hi-yo Silver, gang,' and off we went.

Scott and his mother and the piano were there when we arrived. She was very happy because Scott had asked her to volunteer to be a chaperone at the dance. She was all dressed up and glowing with pride over her darling Scott. Of course, you could say that in a way she didn't know who or even what she was chaperoning, but she was better than nothing.

Scott looked like we did — he didn't stand out too much or anything. I don't think that even if you already knew only one of us was a boy you would have been able to pick out which one.

While we were setting up, I told Scott that he might as well do the M.C. part — you know, introducing the group and announcing the numbers and that sort of thing. That was my job, of course, but on the way to school in the van Steve and the girls had pointed out very firmly that Scott was the logical person to do it this time. I knew that perfectly well, and I also knew that he would be good at it. Of course, the only reason he would be good at it was that the kids at Swanson all knew him, and he was very popular anyway.

Jan intervened hastily. 'It's just for this one time, Tammy, you know that.'

'All right,' I agreed after a while.

Scott acted really pleased, as though it had been my idea. 'Gee thanks, Tammy,' he said.

'Well, you're supposedly the only one of us who goes to Swanson,' I said.

I don't know what I expected when we got there. Did I think someone was going to jump up and yell, 'Hey, that's Tammy Ballantyne with a wig on!'? Probably. Anyway, that didn't happen.

I should have felt on top of the world. After all, it was just over a year ago that they wouldn't let us play, and now here we were. Everyone clapped when Scott announced us; I guess a lot of them must have heard us, or even heard of us, by now.

But I didn't feel on top of the world – I felt funny. Let's face it, we were pretending even more than usual, and it felt strange in the new gear. Besides, it was us they turned down last year, I mean Renee and Caroline and the rest of our real selves, and it wasn't us they were clapping for now – at least they didn't know it was us – they were applauding these other people.

So it didn't feel as good as it should have.

Mr Revson showed up after the first number, to announce that we would be representing Swanson in the Play-off. The kids looked puzzled, naturally, since as far as they knew Scott was the only one in the group who went to Swanson; but Mr Revson stumbled through something about these other, uh, talented young people and inter-school cooperation, and blah blah. I wondered what Miss Vincent had told him. He seemed a little confused, but then he usually does.

The kids looked confused too, but they applauded anyway, because he was the principal and what the heck. I spotted a couple of boys from Scott's old group, though, and they weren't clapping. I suddenly wondered what he'd told them. When I'd asked him about his old group, he'd hurried over that part.

We went into 'Breaking Up Is Hard To Do', one of our most popular numbers, and they started dancing. But as the evening went on, something felt wrong about the mood. I told myself to stop imagining things; it was probably the costumes most of the kids were wearing that made this dance feel different.

Anyway, when our break came we did not mingle with the crowd. In fact, we hid out in the teachers' lounge on the second floor. When we came back, Renee said, 'Oh, look, how cute, a bunch of boys decided to come dressed as hoods.'

That was Renee's idea of a joke. I recognized them right away. These kids always dressed that way, in tight jeans and greasy leather jackets. They thought they were real macho hot stuff. They didn't come to dances, though – not usually. I suppose they were there to try to slip some vodka into the punch, or whatever.

The chaperones were watching them like hawks, and so was Steve, when he wasn't talking to the cute eighth-grade math teacher. They even danced a couple of numbers together. That left only two chaperones to keep an eye on things, and one of them was Scott's mother, who, of course, was mostly watching Scott.

The mood kept getting heavier and heavier. It was affecting us, and our sound was changing. With each number we were sounding a little meaner. And so were the kids.

We decided two more numbers and that's it. While we were figuring out what to do for the next-to-the-last one, the hoods started drifting up to the stand. Then one of them said, 'They look like a bunch of girls to me.'

Without thinking, I said right into the mike, 'Relax, boys. They say that about anybody with clean hair.'

Some of the kids started to laugh. I don't know whether the rest of them would have, because Renee shot me one swift glance and struck up the opening chords of 'Didi Darling'. We'd been planning to save that one for last, but everybody came right in.

We were saved for the moment, but things still weren't quite right. Some of the kids were dancing, some were leaving, and some were waiting around to see what would happen.

I couldn't see Steve anywhere – or the math teacher. Scott's mother was looking upset and nervous, and the other chaperone, Mr Wingate, was looking uncertain.

He's a new English teacher who wears his hair long.

The kids really like him, even the ones who call him 'Relevance Wingate', but I wasn't sure his approach was going to work this time.

It didn't. After 'Didi Darling', the hoods crowded up against the stand. I could see Mr Wingate trying to push through the edges of the crowd, but he wasn't getting very far.

Tom Snyder, a member of Scott's old group, was there too.

'Who are these guys, anyway?' he said.

'Yeah,' said one of the hoods. 'Take off those masks. Come on, Scott, let's see your girlfriends.'

We all froze solid. I couldn't even move my eyes around to look at Scott so I could tell him what a rotten fink he was. Of course I'd always known he was rotten, but I realized in that horrible moment that I'd actually begun to change my mind. I hadn't ever, in my heart, thought he was this bad.

Suddenly there was a shoving and a shrieking. Someone was pushing a very determined path through the crowd. It was Didi.

I don't know what her costume was supposed to be. Some kind of Miss Universe from Outer Space, I suppose. Anyway, there was a silver thing on her head that was all pushed to one side from shoving through the crowd. She stopped in front of the stand and turned to face them.

In a high, breathless voice, she said, 'You just get away from here, you . . . you juvenile delinquents. You leave Ronnie alone!'

This development even froze the Honchos, for a second or two. But it relaxed me so that I could move my eyes. I looked Scott straight in the eye, and he looked back at me, and I suddenly knew he hadn't told.

Then the Honchos started shoving closer to the stand and imitating Didi, squealing 'Ronnie! Leave Ronnie alone!' They headed for her.

From up on the stand, I could still see Mr Wingate trying to get through, but I couldn't hear what he was saying.

As I unplugged my guitar, ready to charge forward and bash the first Honcho who touched her, I thought, 'This is the end of my career, let alone my guitar, dying to defend Didi the Nerd.' But out of the corner of my eye, I saw Monica unplug her bass and Scott grab one of Caroline's cymbals, and I didn't feel nearly as bad as I should have.

22

We heard a dry, crackling noise. It was someone talking. It was Miss Vincent. By then it was the only sound in the gym.

'I have witnessed this entire incident from the gallery,' she said. She was standing right next to Didi. Had she popped up out of the floor, or what?

'Hector Greene, Gary Stanton, and Steven Kleinschmidt, your behaviour has been disgraceful.'

Had there been only three of them?

They stood there, looking down at the floor. Even if the Honchos had been as tough as they thought they were, they couldn't have taken on Miss Vincent. I almost felt sorry for them.

'This group may well be representing not only our school, but the entire district at the Play-off. Hector, Gary, and Steven, you are barred from attending school dances for the rest of the year.'

I never knew Heck Greene's real name was Hector. And they wonder why boys from good homes turn into juvenile delinquents.

Then Miss Vincent announced firmly that the dance was over. The kids looked disappointed, but you could tell they knew this was her way of saying that, even though she'd only punished the ringleaders, she wasn't too happy with the rest of them.

The ringleaders weren't the only ones to get it, either. Miss Vincent had moved around to the side of the stand, and I saw her talking to Mr Wingate and

Miss Mayo, the math teacher. I couldn't hear what she was saying, but from the look on her face and theirs, it had to be 'I'll see you in my office on Monday.' I'd never realized that could happen to teachers, too.

Thanks to Super Vice-Principal, the room was cleared in five minutes, except for Scott's mother and Didi and us. And Didi's mother, who must have come to pick her up and got there for the exciting part. Anyway, she grabbed our knightess in shining armour and said, 'If anything has happened to my Didi at this dreadful school,' while Scott's mother was saying, 'Are you sure you're all right, dear?'

Scott had his piano packed up by this time, and he got himself and the piano and his mother out of there. Meanwhile, Miss Vincent gave Didi's mother a look that said for two cents I'll see *you* in my office on Monday, and she backed down and took Didi away.

'Boy,' I said to Jan, while we were packing up. 'If we had her for a manager, we could go all the way to the top.'

'Speaking of managers,' said Caroline, 'look who's here.'

Steve had come mooching up to the stand. He looked as though he felt almost as bad as he should feel.

'Manager?' said Monica. 'I don't see any manager.'

'Uh, Miss Vincent,' Steve said. 'About Miss Mayo. It was sort of my fault. I mean, we stepped out for a minute, and we got to talking and –'

'Young man,' said Miss Vincent. She didn't yell, exactly, but she got the same effect without yelling, which is much more unpleasant.

'I will deal with Miss Mayo. As for your share of the responsibility for this incident, I have no idea what the duties of a manager are, but I have some idea of what these girls' parents expected when they were entrusted to your care.'

It took me a minute to figure out what she meant, but one thing was obvious right away. For some reason, something popped into my head from this Shakespeare play we read in English. We all had laughed because it sounded so much like modern slang, and it turned out that Shakespeare meant it the same way. This man and this woman are trading incomprehensible wisecracks, and I guess she wins, because somebody says to her: 'You have put him down, lady, you have put him down.' That's what Miss Vincent had done to Steve, and hard. He looked like he was almost ready to cry. It's not very often you see that happen to a big brother, let alone one who's a sophomore in college.

I guess we all felt he'd been punished enough. Anyway, Monica said, 'Hey, manager, do I have to lug this bass out to the van by myself?'

Miss Vincent stuck around to see us off, and while they were loading the stuff in the van, I went back to the gym to talk to her.

'Uh, Miss Vincent,' I said.

She said, 'My friends call me Miss Vincent, without the *uh*.'

I never said she was the easiest person in the world to talk to.

'Miss Vincent,' I said, 'how did you get there? In front of the stand, I mean.'

117

'I came down the back stairs from the gallery, and I used the same door you did. The one just behind the stand.'

'Oh yeah, of course. I see. Uh, I mean, Miss Vincent, there's one other thing I'd like to know. When you — when you put Steve down so hard —'

She smiled at me. 'Yes, Tammy?'

'Well, did you know that — if you did it, then we wouldn't be so mad at him?'

She moved her hand like she was going to pat my head or something, but she didn't. She didn't answer my question, either.

Instead, she said, 'Tammy, you girls have decided to keep up this pretence. I'm not sure you're right, but I'm not sure you're wrong, either. So remember this. Telling the truth of your own free will after the Play-off is good. But if you are found out accidentally, during the Play-off, you will make fools not only of yourselves but of your school and your school district and all of Rocky Point.'

Hoo boy.

Everybody was waiting for me in the van. It was very quiet. When I got in, Steve didn't start the engine right away. Looking straight ahead through the windshield, he said, 'I waited 'til you got here, Tammy, so I could say it to all of you at once. I'm sorry.'

Monica said, 'It's OK.'

'Yeah,' said Renee. 'Just remember to keep your eye on the ball from now on.'

Jan said, 'Steve?'

'What?'

'I know you have to keep up with your college work, and we must be taking up a lot of your time, and your commissions mostly go for gas and stuff . . . Are you sure you want to go on being our manager?'

That's the kind of thing only Jan would think of, but she was right. It just hadn't occurred to me, or to anyone else either.

'Well, Jan,' he said, 'it's true you guys have been kind of taking me for granted. It's also true my commissions are enough to keep Daisy Mae running,' (that was the name of the van) 'and I've had to cut back on my other job. When we started last spring, I did it as a kind of a joke – and to help pay my parents back for their loan. But now – I can't quite imagine life without the Tygers. A reasonable part-time job would seem pretty tame. So, ladies, or gentlemen, as long as you want me, I'll be happy to manage the Tygers.'

'OK by me,' said Monica.

'Me, too,' said Caroline.

'As long as we can't have Miss Vincent,' I said.

'And assuming there's anything left to manage,' added our little Ray of Sunshine.

'What do you mean?' I said.

'Your friend,' said Renee. 'He told.'

I decided to ignore that part about my friend. I could have pointed out that I didn't want him in the first place, but then Renee could have pointed out that I was responsible for his being there in the first place.

So I just said, 'He did not.'

'How do you know?' said Caroline.

'I just know,' I said.

'How come you're on his side all of a sudden?' Monica demanded.

'I'm not — well, I guess I am,' I admitted.

'Why?' said Renee.

'Because he didn't tell,' I said.

'But, Tammy, how do you know he didn't?' said Jan.

'I just know,' I said. The Born Leader is always logical.

Steve started the engine. 'This could go on all night,' he said. 'So, as your manager, I'm giving you some advice. I know I only got there for the end, but it didn't sound to me like anyone really thought you were girls, even the Honchos. If they really do know something, they're going to tell everybody, and if they do, it'll be all over the school Monday morning. So why don't you wait 'til then to make up your minds about Scott?'

'Makes sense to me,' I said.

'That depends,' said Caroline.

'On what?' said Monica.

'If the only thing they know is that we're girls, that's one thing,' Caroline said. 'If they know it was us, you're looking at a ninth-grade dropout — as of first period Monday morning.'

We were all pretty quiet going home.

Going to school Monday morning was not the easiest thing we ever did. In fact, Jan didn't. She told her mother she was sick. Her mother asked her what was wrong and Jan said nothing was, as long as she didn't have to go to school. Jan, as you may have noticed, can be very firm. Cowardly, but firm.

Anyway, she should have gone. Nobody even

wanted to know why we hadn't been at the dance, they were so eager to tell us what we'd missed. I heard some pretty wild stories, too, but nothing anywhere near the truth.

Of course, we got together after school. Only Renee still seemed unconvinced. After all, her two favourite things in the world are total disaster and thinking the worst of somebody. But when Monica pointed out that she'd heard from three different kids that the Tygers had had their shirts torn off, even Renee had to give in.

'I helped to start that one,' Scott said modestly. 'After all,' – he gave us his best innocent-Scott look – 'I was there, wasn't I?'

Caroline looked impressed. 'Scott,' she said, 'you are one sneaky devil.'

Scott smiled at me. 'Tammy,' he said, 'when Steve Greenburg came to me and said, "Hey, is it really true you guys had your shirts torn off?" I knew exactly how you must have felt that time in summer school. You know, when I said I was on to you and the Tygers, and I knew you'd been helping them out? When people make things up for you, it's pretty hard not to be sneaky.'

It was hard not to smile back. In fact, I did.

23

The Born Leader tries to be modest when it is possible, but the fact is, we took the District and the Regional Play-offs. I mean we just *took* them. Even the Regional wasn't that big, of course – there were only four other groups, but two of them were from high schools. Junior-high and high-school rock groups had been put into the same category, although they had made the Regionals smaller than last year, to achieve Maximal Participation.

Participation is very big these days. My eighth-grade teacher had told us she was 'participating in the learning process'. I couldn't figure out what she was talking about, so I asked my father. I shouldn't have. It was at the dinner table, and instead of explaining, he let his dinner get cold while he carried on about sending me to a private school.

Anyway, we won. Or, as Steve put it, we creamed them. And except for two groups that had girl vocalists, they were all boys.

Of course, we had learned to be very foxy about the rest rooms. But once at the Regional, Caroline and I were stuck in our little booths for about twenty minutes while the two girl vocalists talked about which boys were the neatest looking and what kind of make-up to use on stage. They thought some of the Tygers were pretty cute, especially Scott and Ron, but they agreed that we must be very stuck up. We still were not very good at mingling with the crowd.

I was just bored and worried, but Caroline was really upset. 'Tammy,' she said afterward, 'they're supposed to be musicians, and all they talked about was boys and make-up.'

'And Beverly's really good, too,' I said. She was one of the girls in the rest room. She wasn't the only one, either. Some of those groups had one or two really talented guys in them; they just didn't have it together. Then there was this high-school group that Beverly sang with – they called themselves the Hot Shots. They might have beaten us out if we hadn't had to do three numbers. They had two that were really good, but on the third one, when it was between our two groups, it was obvious right away that they hadn't really practised. By this time, we had six or seven numbers down solid; so, you see, it pays to work with a Born Leader.

After the Regional we all felt very good – even Renee, I think, although the only way you could tell was that she didn't make so many sneering remarks.

After the regular Wednesday afternoon rehearsal, we met to discuss our new material. We had already decided to add one new number: the Play-off was during Christmas vacation, and one was all we would have time for if we were going to get it right. I was all set for lots of democratic discussion and nobody agreeing, with me cleverly switching sides if it looked like they *were* all about to agree. Then I would introduce my suggestion (I was determined to do 'Twist and Shout'), and everybody would vote for it because they were tired of arguing and didn't want to vote for each other's.

It didn't work out that way.

The first thing that happened was that Jan said, 'I don't want to do just another oldie. I think we should do a song that – that says something.'

Monica had always wanted us to do a message song, but Jan? It wasn't like her to start the discussion, much less to have an idea like that. Or was it? She is basically a serious person, and this fall she is taking English from Mr Wingate. When I remind you that he is known to his students as Relevance Wingate, you will understand why I should have seen this coming. His favourite phrase is 'social relevance'. The basic idea seemed to be that if you're writing or singing or whatever, you should do it about something you object to. Anyway, now that Jan had brought it up, I could see a determined look in Monica's eye. And the others looked very interested.

'Listen,' I said, hoping the kind but firm approach would work, 'social relevance is college. It is even high school, maybe, but it is not junior high. Nobody in junior high is socially relevant. At least nobody at Swanson.'

'Maybe we should do a protest song about how we're not socially relevant,' said Renee. I couldn't tell if she was sneering or not; I couldn't even tell if she was on my side.

'Monica is,' said Scott. 'She's black.'

I was getting confused. 'Are we supposed to object to that?' I asked.

The rest of them just looked at me like I was a dummy and went on as though I hadn't said anything.

'I think Sebastian Fox is relevant, too,' said Monica.

Caroline said, 'I know, Monica.' (Know what? I had

no idea what they were talking about, which any Born Leader will tell you is a very bad fix to be in.) 'But we can hardly sing a protest song about how we're forced to dress up like boys.'

'No way,' said Scott.

I must have looked as baffled as I felt, because Caroline explained patiently: 'Look, Tammy. We have to pretend that we're boys. Monica has to tell everyone she's black.'

'Because if I don't, they might think I'm pretending not to be,' Monica added.

I could almost understand, but not quite. So I back-tracked.

'OK,' I said. 'Our new number will be a protest song. It'll be relevant.'

'Relevant to what?' asked Renee.

I was ready for her. Your Born Leader thinks very fast. While I was trying to figure out what they were talking about, I had also been thinking that in the Play-off we were going to be up against high-school groups and at least a few of them would probably have social relevance songs.

'Relevant to us,' I said. 'Relevant to everybody. We'll do "Blowin' in the Wind".'

It wasn't the song I had wanted to do in the first place, but it's pretty. And at least it was my idea.

'A nice safe protest everything song,' sneered Renee.

'That's the kind that makes the charts,' I retorted. 'I don't mean that we'll ever get to make a record, let alone the charts, but that's what people like and that's what the judges will like, and we'll win.'

They all looked at me as if they were hypnotized. I stared back at them. Then Jan hiccupped.

'Tammy,' she said, 'that's not why we're going to do the song.'

'That's not why we're going to do "Blowin' in the Wind"?' I was caught off guard. Jan is so easy to hypnotize that I hadn't been concentrating on her.

'No,' she said. 'I think we should do an original song. My song.'

Jan? Write a song? Now we were all staring at her. What had gotten into Jan lately?

'It's just an idea, really, and a few words, but if you and Renee would help, I think it could be a song. And we could do it in the Play-off.'

She wouldn't tell us any more then, so we all agreed that Renee, Jan, and I would get together Friday night and write this song. Then we'd meet on Saturday afternoon, as usual, and decide if we should learn it for the Play-off.

We worked hard on it, and what we ended up with was 'Let Me Out'. It's Jan's song, really, even though all she brought over on Friday was a kind of tune and some lines:

> *I'm locked inside a thing,*
> *Something I'm supposed to be.*
> *It walks, it talks, it even sings –*
> *But it doesn't act like me.*

Two original songs, and one of them was even relevant. I figured we had it made.

24

Mom and Dad, who had to be with us because otherwise, according to the rules, we had to stay at the Y.M.C.A. with the rest of the boys, had reserved rooms at a motel practically around the corner from the auditorium where the Play-off was being held. That would be a big help with the rest room question. We picked up the schedule and some more announcements at the Y, then we saw what the real problem was going to be. The Play-off lasted four days – and there was a getting-to-know-you party that night, an indoor barbecue, and two more dances.

My mother picked up the social events calendar. 'Charles, look at this!' she said.

My father glanced at it. 'What's an indoor barbecue?' he said.

'Never mind that,' she said. 'The point is do we have to chaperone the girls at all these events?'

'Not me, you don't,' said Renee. 'I'm not going.'

The rest of us agreed with that, except Scott, of course. He was really looking forward to them, you could tell.

But everybody had to attend the get-together that night. We saw a lot of girls there, which surprised me, but it turned out that most of them weren't contestants. They were from Vernon, the state capital, and they had been invited 'so you boys will have someone to dance with,' said Dr Vandevere, who seemed to be running the show. He was not an M.D., this one. Just the head of the state musical education department, when I didn't even know there was one.

His welcoming speech seemed like about an hour's worth of blah blah blah about how he wanted us all to have a valuable social learning experience and how he hoped everyone would stay on for the finals, even if they were eliminated in the first round, as Jan was secretly hoping we would be. I pricked up my ears when he mentioned that there were also some girls in the Play-off.

Jan grabbed my hand. 'Not us, you fool, he doesn't mean us!' I whispered, frantically trying to get my hand back and praying I was right.

Just then he was saying, 'And now, to start off our introductions, let me present these charming young ladies from St Mary's School in Evantown, the Belles of St Mary's.'

Jan let me have my hand back.

St Mary's is a boarding school where very rich girls go so they can tell each other how classy they are. Naturally, they would have an all-girl group. I didn't see what there was to make such a fuss about. They were all sort of tanned and sleek-looking.

'Now that we've had ladies first,' beamed Dr Vandevere, 'let's all come up and introduce ourselves.'

He called out the groups one by one, and then each member went up and said his name and age into the microphone. Our turn started out smoothly. Up on the stage I felt like Tommy, almost. We all agreed that the terrifying part wasn't up on stage, it was down there with the kids. Usually. Renee practically swaggered up to the mike. 'My name is Ron Austin,' she began.

'Ronnie!' shrieked several voices.

Of course. We should have known.

'Well, well,' chuckled Dr Idiot. 'It seems one of our budding stars has a fan club already. I guess we know one boy who's going to have a good time at the Play-off.'

Renee just stared at him like a dummy. Since I was the only one who hadn't introduced myself yet, I ploughed her out of the way and said my name and shoved us all down the stairs.

There was only one more group to be introduced, and from where we were I could see Didi and her little group working their way towards us. Scott and I decided to head them off. Jan was hiccupping hysterically, Renee was still like a zombie, and Caroline and Monica kept whispering to each other, 'I guess we know *one* boy who's going to have a good time,' and giggling. So we were the only ones.

We met Didi and one of her friends about halfway across the room. She was glowing, as usual.

'Hi, Scott. Hi, Tommy! Guess what? My cousin lives here in Vernon, so I came up to stay with her and see you guys in the Play-off.'

Not that it makes any difference about your cousin, I thought. If the Play-off were held at the North Pole it would turn out there was an International Nerds Convention there at the same time and there you'd be, screeching 'Ronnie!'

'Tommy,' said Didi, 'I'd like you to meet Charlene.'

'Hi,' I said.

In the pause that followed, I realized they'd put on some records, and the kids were beginning to dance.

Didi was looking around for Ronnie. Charlene was looking at me. Then all of a sudden there was dear, wonderful Steve.

'Hello there, girls,' he beamed at them. 'I hope you're not going to encourage the boys to break training. Time for us to be getting back.'

Didi looked puzzled, and I couldn't blame her.

'But all the others are staying,' she said.

Steve looked at her kindly. 'Didi,' he said gently, 'you want to see Ron and the other boys go all the way to the top in the Play-off, don't you?'

'Oh, yes!' she breathed.

'Well, that's how you get there,' Steve explained. 'Keep in shape. Get plenty of sleep.'

Charlene looked him straight in the eye. 'It's seven-thirty,' she said.

'We always practise for two hours before we go to bed,' I said quickly. I knew Scott wanted to stay, but he didn't say anything.

'The other boys are waiting out in the van,' said Steve. 'And, Didi, Ron wanted me to tell you how much he appreciated your cheering for him like that.'

Didi looked very pleased. 'Oh, gosh,' was all she said.

Steve continued. 'But we feel that – well, it might make the other groups jealous, and the judges might think we were trying to pressure them, so maybe if from now on you could be a little less enthusiastic?'

'Oh, sure,' said Didi, 'I would never do anything to hurt Ron!'

Poor Renee.

25

We decided that we were more than happy to let Scott go to the rest of the social events by himself or with Steve. But we made him promise not to tell us about them, because it did sound like fun – meeting all these other kids who were musicians just like us. Jan didn't really mind, since she's shy around strangers anyway, and Renee didn't mind at all, since the thought of meeting Didi again turned her green. Monica and Caroline were sort of wistful, though, especially Caroline, who kept saying 'all those *boys*', until we made her stop. I told myself I didn't mind, since the important thing was winning. I even made myself believe it. Besides, maybe we should stay in training; this was stiffer competition than we'd ever faced before.

There was one group I was curious about – the all-girls one, of course. They were scheduled for the first round, at one o'clock the next day, and we weren't on until three. I went over early to catch their set. They had a very good sound – sort of a Latin beat, but not too heavy. Of course they had fabulous equipment, but they were also really together. Their lead guitarist was almost as good as Renee, and she was more relaxed on stage. Why shouldn't she be? She didn't have Didi. And their lead singer was really good, better than me, if you want to know the truth.

Anyway, it was clear that they practised hard. Maybe there's nothing else to do at a girls' boarding school. Even though it was warm in there, and I felt silly keeping my windbreaker on, to say nothing of how hot it was under that wig, I stuck it out; after their set I went backstage where they had refreshments. Any contestants who didn't feel like watching the others could hang out there. I didn't see any of the other Belles, but I did see their lead guitarist, so I went over and introduced myself. I told her I really liked their music.

'Thanks,' she said. She didn't sound too enthusiastic, after all, she was in tenth grade, and she probably wasn't very interested in ninth-grade boys, but she had a nice smile.

'I was just wondering if you've ever had a problem – because you're girls, you know.'

She gave me a polite, blank look.

'I mean . . . we had this girls' rock group at our school and – well, nobody wanted to hire them for dances because they were girls. So they –'

Now she looked puzzled. 'So they what?' she asked.

'They disbanded,' I finished lamely.

She said, 'Well, of course Swanson is a *public* school, isn't it?'

It was my turn to stare at her.

'I mean,' she said, 'maybe it would be harder at a public – I mean a coed school. But we played at two Sweet Sixteen parties, and once we even did a coming out.'

Coming out? Coming out of where? The only thing I could think of was jail, but St Mary's isn't that kind of school at all.

'And we never had any trouble,' she went on. 'So if your girls' group had to disband, I guess they just didn't have what it takes.'

It took me a second to remember she wasn't talking about us, or at least, she didn't know she was.

I pulled myself together and changed the subject.

'Do you girls have any original material?' I asked.

'Of course we do,' she said. 'We're saving our original number for the semi-finals.'

She was that sure they were going to make the semi-finals. After all, they were only competing with groups from public schools.

It was very hard not to retort, 'Oh yeah, we'll have one for the semi-finals and another one for the finals, little Miss Has-what-it-takes!'

I managed not to say that, only I couldn't think of anything to say instead; but I was saved. She glanced over my shoulder and her face lit up.

'Hi, Scott!' she said.

'Hi, Eileen.'

We'd been there twenty-four hours, and he probably knew every girl in the Play-off. Anyway, here was one ninth-grade boy she didn't seem to mind. Knowing Scott, he'd probably convinced her that he was a child prodigy and a senior at Harvard.

'Hey, Tommy,' he said. 'We're on next. Time to set up.'

As soon as we were out in the corridor, I said, 'Scott, we don't have to set up for ages yet. And do you know what she said?'

'I heard part of it. And I've talked to her, so I can imagine the rest.'

The door he had taken us to led to a hallway that seemed to have no one in it.

'The thing is there's something I have to tell you.'

'OK,' I said, not very surprised. It couldn't be a coincidence that we'd come to the one spot in the whole building where you could be alone. But now that we had this amazing privacy, he didn't seem to know what to do with it. I waited. But all he did was take a pack of gum out of his pocket, slide out a piece, and look at it.

'I didn't know you chewed gum.'

'I quit when I joined the Tygers,' he said, 'but I still need a stick every once in a while, especially when I'm nervous. You want some?'

I'd already seen the pack; it was Juicyfruit. When I shook my head, he took out another pack. 'Now I could say,' he said as he offered me a stick of Spearmint which I accepted, 'I could say that I could tell just by looking at you that you were a Spearmint kind of girl.'

'You probably have.'

'As a matter of fact, I know you like Spearmint because that's what you liked in fourth grade.'

We unwrapped our gum, leaned back against the wall, and chewed in silence for a minute. It was the most relaxed I'd felt in a long time.

'What I was going to tell you is this: when I – OK, when I blackmailed you into letting me join the Tygers, it's true that I wanted to because it was a better group than mine, but I also wanted to get even with you.'

'For what?' I said, really wanting to know. I couldn't think of a thing I'd done to him.

Scott gave me an uncertain, sideways look. 'I don't

know. For having a better group because you were more in charge. Maybe I pretended a little bit, so I could get the others on my side.'

I swallowed my gum. 'A little bit!'

'I've felt different for a long time,' Scott said, 'ever since I asked Renee how you could dislike me so much and still tell me to my face I was a good musician. She said you had talent, and you didn't mind if other people had more. That's why you were such a good leader.'

'Renee said that?'

'Tammy, let's tell Dr Vandevere, let's tell whoever's in charge. We'll beat the Belles fair and square. I'll wear a skirt if I have to.'

I thought it over. I really did. I said 'No.'

He looked so discouraged, or anyway his back did, which was all I could see as he trudged away down the hall, that I called his name loud enough for him to turn around. Then I had to look down for a minute to make sure I really meant what I was going to say. I did, but it was hard.

'Scott, I'm glad that you joined the group.'

When I looked up, he was staring at me. I had never noticed before what colour his eyes are, since it had never mattered.

'See you on stage in twenty minutes,' I said.

26

For our set we did 'Breaking Up Is Hard To Do', 'She Was Just Seventeen', and for our final number, an old Everly Brothers song that I discovered called 'Gone, Gone, Gone'. We were sensational.

The other kids sure thought so. By our third number almost everyone had come in from the back room. They were practically dancing in the aisles, and at the end they applauded like crazy. I was higher than a kite. I wasn't sure how much the judges counted audience appeal, but after a response like that we had to be a cinch for the semi-finals. Furthermore, the Born Leader had once again been proved right. Right, right, right! The others hadn't even wanted to learn that song.

Then Doom came charging down a crowded aisle in the person of Mary Beth Hansen. She had the biggest mouth in all of Swanson Junior High, and the pit of my stomach knew she was going to recognize us. Don't ask me how it knew, but it did.

'Scott!' I hissed.

Scott was pretending to put away his piano, but mostly was just basking in the applause. He looked over at me.

'We'll get the piano. You get down there and head off Mary Beth.'

'Who?' he said.

'Mary Beth! There, halfway down the centre aisle!'

It seemed to me like it took him ten minutes to find

her. 'Oh, I see her,' he said finally. 'But so what? She doesn't –'

'Do it!' I screamed quietly.

He did it.

The rest of the group were looking at me and Scott and each other.

'Tammy –' Jan began.

'Shut up and let's get packed and get out of here,' I said. 'I'll explain later.'

Scott met Mary Beth at the end of the aisle, almost underneath the stage where she couldn't see us. It had quieted down, so we could even hear some of what they were saying.

'Honeychild,' said Scott (I rolled my eyes at Monica), 'what are you doing here?'

'I have this friend who lives up here, so naturally Peggy and I just had to come up and root for the home team. You boys were just fabulous!'

'When you're hot, you're hot,' said Scott with his usual modesty.

'Aren't you going to introduce me to the others? Like your leader, Tommy, what's his last name?'

'Smith,' he replied promptly.

Right on, I thought. There are times when speed counts more than originality.

'Oh,' she said. 'You know, I'm sure I've seen him somewhere. Besides the Halloween dance, I mean. And the bass player –'

'Maybe you saw them at the Midsummer Fling,' Scott suggested.

'No, it was somewhere else. Somewhere like –'

'Let's go get a pizza and figure it out,' said Scott.

So I didn't have to explain after all.

Caroline said, 'I'm going back to the motel.'

The others agreed that it had been a tiring day, so I stayed by myself to wait for the announcement of the semi-finalists.

There were more groups to sit through, and then they didn't make the announcement from the stage, for some reason. They posted this tiny little typed list, and we all had to crowd around it to see.

We were on it, of course. Along with the Belles of St Mary's and five other groups. Three of us would make it to the finals.

I raced back to the motel and burst into our room.

'Hello there, semi-finalists!' I cried.

No one even turned to look at me except Jan, who said, 'Tammy, you've got to talk her out of it. We can't find Steve or Scott, and your parents are out at a museum somewhere, and she won't listen to us.'

My brain took in what my eyes were seeing. Caroline in a slip. And stockings. And high heels. And eyeshadow. Not George. No way.

'What . . . ?' I started to ask.

'I'm going to that barbecue. And you're not going to stop me. And no one's going to recognize me.'

'But —'

'If anyone asks, which they won't, I'm George's sister.'

'What about Mary Beth?' I said.

'If I run into her, I'll just tell her I had to come and root for the home team. Anyway, wait 'til you see me in this dress.'

'Dress? You brought a dress?'

'I packed it in a separate box and then hid it up on the closet shelf.'

The Born Leader knows a determined person when she sees one. So did the others, I guess. We just stood or sat where we were while Caroline dragged a chair in front of the closet, slid open the doors, and climbed up on it. She glanced down and suddenly something went wrong with the high heels. She drew in her breath like she was going to scream, and then fell off the chair instead. Monica and Renee caught her.

There was a scuffling noise behind the suitcases on the closet floor, and someone stood up. A girl with blonde curls and enormous eyes, which were staring straight at Caroline.

Didi was the first one to break the silence, in a kind of squeaky whisper.

'George!' she said.

27

Caroline was the first one to move. She went over to the bed and grabbed her bathrobe.

'What are you staring at?' she said. 'Haven't you ever seen a girl before?'

'And what are you doing in our closet?' said Monica.

A good question, but Didi didn't answer it. She transferred her stare to Monica and said, 'Sebastian. Your hair.'

Oh wow. Monica had taken off her Michael Jackson wig, and her hair was hanging loose around her shoulders.

'I'm letting it grow,' she said.

Didi ignored that, too. She was looking around the room at all of us.

'Are . . . do you? . . .'

'Didi,' said Renee slowly and clearly, 'we are girls. We are all girls.'

'Except Scott,' put in Jan. 'Scott is a boy.' She said it kind of hopefully, as though it would make things better.

'You can come out of the closet now,' said Renee.

Didi climbed over the suitcases and walked over to one of the beds and sat down on it, all without taking her eyes off Renee.

'You're a girl,' she said.

'Yes,' said Renee. 'I'm a girl, my name is Renee Austin, I'm thirteen, and I'm in the ninth grade at

Swanson Junior High. Is there anything else you want to know?'

Didi stared at her for a few more seconds. Then she giggled. Then she started to laugh. She was laughing so hard she fell over on her side on the bed, then slipped down to the floor.

We sat there like dummies, looking at each other and at Didi, who was sitting on the floor with her back against the bed, chortling, 'I'll stop in a minute, but it is so f-f-funny,' and off she went again.

Finally Jan went to the bathroom and got a glass of water and gave it to her, ignoring Caroline's advice to dump it over her head. Didi drank it and calmed down.

'The thing is,' she said, 'my mother was worried about me because I wasn't dating any boys. I don't know why I should be, I'm only thirteen. So I was talking to a friend, and she said that she'd had the same problem, and what you do is get a big crush on some rock or movie star and then you don't actually have to do anything and your mother decides you're normal and gets off your back. I was going to do Matt Dillon, but then I saw the Tygers. And you had this song with my name in it. I decided that if I did Matt Dillon she would just tell her friends how cute it was, but if I did one of you it would be a real live boy, and she'd be kind of worried and annoyed, and it would serve her right.'

This was one very cunning nerd.

'I picked Ron because he was the meanest looking,' she continued, 'and it really worked. It bugged her. Then I started to get interested. You were all so mysterious. And then that night at the Halloween dance, I jumped in there because I could see you were in trouble, and I just knew there was something funny going on.' Her shoulders started to shake again. 'And after the dance, she said – my mom, I mean – bring me some more water – she said, "But my dear, you don't really know anything *about* this boy".'

Well, it was pretty funny. The only one who didn't laugh was Caroline, who was still in a huff. I guess she's not used to being stared at like she was the creature from the black lagoon.

'As long as you're telling us the story of your life,' she said, 'maybe you could bring us up to date. Like what were you doing in our closet?'

Ah, yes. Why hadn't I, with all my famous instincts, noticed that Didi wasn't there at the performance today?

'I wanted to find out more about you guys. I knew you wouldn't be here this afternoon, so I got your room number from the office, and then I sneaked in and hid when the maid left the door open for a minute. I didn't have time to look around very much. I didn't expect you back so soon.'

'What were you looking for?' said Renee.

For the first time, Didi looked uncomfortable.

'You made such a *secret* of everything. I thought you might be – pushing drugs or something.'

'Didi,' I said, 'do you read Nancy Drew mysteries?'

She wouldn't look at me. 'I used to.'

Hah, I thought. You used to, like I used to. I had to make a first-class scene to keep my mother from giving my collection of 175 Nancy Drews to the Salvation Army. She kept saying, 'But why do you want them? You don't read them anymore, do you?' and I didn't feel like admitting that occasionally I go back and reread some of my favourites. So, instead, I said, what about when Dad's mom threw out his collection of Superman comics, which he's figured out would be worth thousands of dollars today? I don't know if she really bought that, but she let me keep them.

'Anyway,' Jan said, 'now that we know what you were doing in our closet, I guess you want to know why we're pretending to be boys.'

Didi looked surprised.

'That's obvious,' she said. 'Who would hire you if they knew you were a bunch of girls?'

This was not a nerd at all.

'So you won't tell?' said Monica.

'Of course not,' said Didi indignantly. 'I'll be right there at the semi-finals and the finals, yelling "Ronnie!"'

'Actually, I don't think you need to do that any-more,' said Renee.

'It might look funny if I stopped now,' Didi pointed out.

I'd figured that at least one good thing had come out of this — we wouldn't hear anything more about Caroline going to the barbecue. But I was wrong. She decided to go as George. 'You can be my date,' she said to Didi. They both giggled so much while Caroline was getting dressed that I was sure they'd blow it at the dance, but they didn't.

When my parents came back and Steve and Scott showed up, we told them about Didi.

Scott was surprised, of course, but not as much as the rest of us.

'I was the one who spent the most time talking to her,' he pointed out, 'and there was something that didn't exactly fit. She was so curious – not just about Renee, but about all of us. And some of the answers I invented were pretty off-the-wall, but she never batted an eyelash. I was beginning to think nobody could be that dumb. It'll sure be a relief not having to do that anymore.' He also agreed that it would look funny if she and her friends stopped screaming 'Ronnie'.

In any case, they didn't. During the semi-finals Didi and her crew were worse – or better – than ever. It made me wonder if she wasn't – well, revenge is a strong word, but after all, we had been putting her on.

It turned out to be contagious. Pretty soon there must have been at least ten girls screeching 'Ronnie!' Didi was the big expert on Ronnie and the rest of the group, of course, so if there was anything the others wanted to know, she'd make up an answer on the spot. She was good at it, too. We voted five to one to make her National President of the Tommy and the Tygers fan club. Guess who voted no.

We did 'Didi Darling' for our original in the semi-finals. The other kids really liked it, although our faithful spy Didi reported that the judges hadn't seemed too impressed. We made it to the finals, along with the Belles and a boys' high-school group.

'Don't worry,' I assured the others. 'The judges are going to love "Let Me Out". It's got protest and social relevance, and those things go over very big. They show we're, you know, serious. Besides, we'll be the only ones with two original numbers. The Belles seem to be saving theirs for the finals.'

'They are,' said Didi. 'I talked to their vocalist at the barbecue, and she said when they'd seen who the other semi-finalists were going to be, they realized they were going to make the finals, so they thought they might as well save it.'

'I hope a guitar string breaks in the middle of a number and they forgot to bring spares,' said Monica.

'They probably have a maid for that,' sneered Renee.

In the finals each group was supposed to do two numbers, then they would start again, and each group would do one more. The boys' group, or I should say the *other* boys' group, went first. I knew after their first number that they had been included just so there would be three finalists. They were good, but not as good as we were. The Belles played second. Their original song was a disco number, and the words were what I think is called social satire. It was supposed to be making fun of people who wanted to protest and change things, but if you ask me they were really making fun of everybody who wasn't just like them.

'Of course, I want us to win,' I whispered to Monica, 'but I also really want them to lose.'

'You and me both,' Monica whispered back.

But the problem was, they were really good musicians. They were as good as we were. It was going to be us or them.

28

We saved 'Let Me Out' for our final number, and we gave it everything we had. There was lots of applause, but we couldn't tell about the judges, who were way in the back as usual. There were three of them – Dr Vandevere of course, Hank Thomas, who I could tell by his little red beard was a local celebrity – a disc jockey, and Miranda Oliver. Miranda Oliver had had a hit record in 1958 or 1959. She sells real estate now.

When we had finished, Dr Boom-boom, as he was known behind his back, came up on stage and thanked everybody. He explained that the judges had a tough decision to make and blah-blah-blah. He said the winners would be officially announced at the dance that night, when all three finalist groups would play. What I couldn't figure out how to ask was whether the winners would be notified before the official announcement.

I didn't have to. We were packing the van when someone came out to the parking lot and said Dr V. wanted to see me in his office. I couldn't even look at the others. I just went.

All three of the judges were there, with these strange expressions on their faces. I couldn't tell from looking at them whether we had won or not. We must have won, I told myself. Why else would they want to see me? Because they had found out, that's why else.

'Sit down, Tommy,' boomed Dr V.

I sat, trying not to faint with relief.

'Well, as you young folks say, I've got some good news and some bad news.'

I guessed I was supposed to say something, but I couldn't think of anything, so I just stared at him.

'That last song of yours indicated to us that you and the other boys have a real sense of social responsibility,' he boomed. 'That's one reason we decided to explain to you. We feel sure you'll be mature enough to understand.' He paused again.

I wanted to scream, 'Understand what, you dodo? Did we win or didn't we?' but of course that was out of the question, so I just sat there and tried to look mature and socially responsible. He went on.

'Both your group and the Belles of St Mary's were so good that we couldn't make up our minds. So we . . .'

The way he kept pausing and glancing over at Miranda Oliver gave me the feeling that whatever he was trying to say wasn't his idea. He did that so much I finally looked at her myself. She was very good-looking, for someone who had had a hit record in 1958 or 1959. I bet she sells a lot of real estate.

Dr V. decided to start again. 'It's always been difficult for girls – uh, female musicians to get a fair chance, even at this level.'

I didn't want to let myself see what was coming.

'So we decided that, with all the changes taking place today, maybe it's time to give the girls a break.'

Now there was no way I could not understand. When I got myself together again enough to listen to him, he was saying, '. . . so we hoped you'd understand our decision.'

'I understand, sir,' said someone, apparently me.

He beamed at me. 'I was sure you would.' He glanced over at the disc jockey. 'Now for the good news.'

I stood up. 'Excuse me, sir,' I said. 'I can't talk any more right now. I have to go tell the others.'

'You mean the other boys in your group?' said Miranda Oliver.

I looked at her. Just for a second I had an odd feeling that she knew – but that didn't make any sense, and anyway I was too numb to care, so I just said, 'Yes, ma'am,' and got myself out the door somehow. My mother was waiting on the other side.

'The others are back at the motel,' she said. 'I didn't know what the judges wanted you for, so I thought I'd wait for you, just in case.'

The next thing I knew we were in our car in the parking lot. I cried for half an hour. Then we went back to tell the others.

29

'Let me get this straight,' said Caroline. 'They couldn't choose between us, so they chose the Belles because they were girls?'

'That's right,' I said.

'But that's so unfair!' said Monica. 'If any girls ever had an even break, it's them. We're the ones who had to –'

'I know,' I said.

We were all gathered in my parents' room – Steve, my parents, and the others.

'Couldn't you tell them?' said my father.

'We can't,' I said.

I looked at Scott and took a deep breath. 'And there's something you should know, which is that it was my own stubborn, stupid fault. If I'd listened to –'

'Tammy!'

Scott interrupted so loudly that everyone gave him a surprised look. He seemed surprised himself. 'It was your stubbornness and your stupid idea that got the Tygers this far.'

Renee said, 'Of course we can't tell now. Tommy and the Tygers came to this Play-off, and Tommy and the Tygers are leaving it.'

'Right on,' said Monica. 'We're going to play at that dance tonight, and we're gonna play those Belles right into the ground!'

'Right back to the belfry!' shouted Jan.

That's when I found out that the Born Leader is only as good as her people.

My mother said, 'Then let's –' She didn't get a chance to finish, because someone was pounding on the door.

It was Didi, looking absolutely radiant.

'Sebastian,' she said, 'get your wig on!'

'Didi,' said Caroline, 'the dance isn't for a couple of hours yet. Anyway, we lost.'

'I know that,' said Didi, as though we'd just told her it was raining or something. 'Listen. I've been talking to Hank Thomas.'

'The DJ?' I asked. 'The judge with red hair and a little beard?'

'Yes,' said Didi. 'Now shut up. He couldn't find any of you, so he told me he wants you to make a record!'

'Didi,' said my father, 'is this some kind of a joke?'

'No,' said Didi. 'I thought they'd let you know in advance if you'd won, so I went back to the auditorium a little while ago, and there was that DJ, Hank Thomas, and he said, "You seem to be the local groupie" (she giggled), "do you know where I can find Tommy and the Tygers?" So of course I said no, and he told me if I saw you to tell you to get in touch with him – he gave me this card with his phone number. He said you'd disappeared so fast he hadn't had a chance to talk to you. "The kid took it kinda hard," was what he said; that's how I knew you hadn't won. And he said for you to be sure to play "Didi Darling" at the dance tonight – he has this friend in the record business, and he's going to bring him!'

My father took the card and went to call Hank

Thomas. While he was gone, we all passed the time trying to cure Jan's hiccups. He was gone about a half hour and by the time he got back I almost had hiccups myself.

'I met Hank Thomas, and his friend, Mr Martinelli,' my father said.

'Well?' I demanded. 'Is he for real?'

'I wouldn't exactly say that,' said my father, 'but he seems to be on the level about wanting to record you, *if* he thinks you're good enough, so —'

'Don't get your hopes up,' we all chorused. My dad said we should change our name to the Smart Alecks.

Jan still had the hiccups. We tried everything: sugar, glasses of water. No results. And time was getting short.

'Our big break,' I said bitterly, 'and you've got the hiccups.'

Renee said maybe we could make her a part of the rhythm section. I suggested that Renee could take her sense of humour and wrap it around her neck and strangle herself. Just one big, happy family.

'I know one that always works,' said Didi, 'only it's kind of drastic. But with forty-five minutes 'til showtime . . . We'll have to stand her on her head in a tub of ice water.'

My father headed for the door. 'There's an ice machine next to the office,' he said. The rest of us headed for the bathroom.

'NO!' screamed Jan. There was a long, tense silence, broken by a collective sigh of relief.

'Didi,' I said, 'if there's ever anything we can do for you . . .'

'Just sock it to 'em tonight,' said Didi. 'See you at the dance.' And she left.

Of course we did try not to get our hopes up, but just knowing Mr Martinelli was there made it easier to get through the announcement of the winners. The Belles weren't surprised, naturally. They had just assumed they would win. Afterward, while the second runners-up were playing, their lead guitarist said to me, 'I'm really glad you guys came in second. You deserved it.' And she thought she was being nice!

I think I would have spotted Mr Martinelli even if he hadn't been with Hank Thomas. I could see what my father meant about not being sure if he was for real. His clothes looked strange but expensive. I mean you could tell they were supposed to look that way, even if you couldn't tell why. While we were between numbers, I saw him talking to my father.

We got an enormous hand from the other kids when we finished. I think they liked us better than the Belles, but a lot of these kids had been in the Play-off too, so it could have been personal, not musical. Personally, it would be hard not to like anybody better than the Belles.

My father came over after we had finished. 'Boys,' he said, 'I'd like you to meet Mr Martinelli.'

'Call me Ralph,' said Mr M. 'Well, boys, you're even better than Hank said you were. I've got enough on tape to take back to New York, and if they like it as much as I do, you boys and your folks will be hearing from us.'

I almost blew it. I barely stopped myself in time from

throwing my arms around good ol' Ralph and giving him a great big kiss.

My mother was the one who answered him. She kept looking back at Jan. 'That's wonderful news,' she said briskly. 'Now these boys have had a long day, and it's time they were all home and in bed.' She glanced uncertainly at the clock. It was eight-fifteen. 'We're making a *very* early start tomorrow,' she added firmly.

'We can't leave now,' said Scott. 'George has to have a farewell dance with Didi.'

'Oh yes,' said Caroline, trying to look mournful and romantic. 'I promised. After all, we may never meet again.'

Mom glared, but what could she do? Anyway, Mary Beth Hansen showed up, so Scott didn't have much choice about a farewell dance with her.

Monica was obviously feeling much too good to sit still. 'Come on, Mrs B.,' she said to my mother, 'let's have us a farewell dance.'

Mom said, 'But I can't –'

'Sure you can,' said Monica, beaming at her. 'It's easy. I'll show you.'

Mom caught on fast, and she turned out to be a very good dancer for someone her age. She looked like she was enjoying herself, too.

Hank excused himself to go dance with somebody, so that left Dad and me and Jan and Renee to talk to Mr Martinelli. If Mom hadn't wanted to dance because then Jan wouldn't have anyone to stare at her, she shouldn't have worried. Renee had taken it over, and she was giving it steel. Come to think of it, Jan did look a little pale, but who wouldn't with people staring at her like that?

Mr Martinelli said, 'I'm glad you could stick around for a minute. If we record "Didi Darling", what have you got for the flip side?'

'We do have another original,' I said.

'Like this one?' he asked.

Renee and Jan were busy with their snake and rabbit act, so it was obviously up to me to do the talking.

'No,' I answered, 'it's different. It's – slower. Actually, it's kind of a protest song.'

'Glad to hear it,' he said. 'Protest always sells if you package it right. When you boys get home, why don't you tape it and send it along?'

'Sure,' I said. You never stay in heaven for very long. The Belles were playing now – the big winners came last, of course, and after that it was going to be disco – and they were sounding even better than they had in the finals. It was like they knew the other kids had wanted us to win, and they were going to show them. We'd moved pretty far away from the stand so we'd be able to talk, but of course you could still hear them loud and clear. I had a sneaking, horrible fear. Ralph Martinelli discovers the Belles of St Mary's. They zoom to the top of the charts. 'I went there to hear another group,' he tells the reporters. They always say that.

Trying to sound casual, I said, 'What do you think of the winners?'

'Them?' He shrugged. 'They're OK. Hey listen, kids, Hank told me about you guys losing out because they're girls. Don't let it get to you. It's still the boys that sell the records.'

Jan made the first sound she'd made since we left the stand. She hiccupped.

30

We decided to celebrate back at the motel with two Sam's Super-Enormos from the terrific place around the corner. My parents left money for the pizza and went off to celebrate by themselves in a civilized restaurant. When I asked Dad what that meant, he explained cheerfully, 'Any place so expensive that none of the other customers will be under thirty-five. But don't take it personally.' So everyone was happy.

Except Jan. She was looking pale. She's usually a quiet sort of person but she hadn't said anything at all for quite a while.

'Jan,' I said, 'what's the matter? And Renee, why were you and Mom taking turns trying to hypnotize her back there at the dance?'

'Nobody was trying to hypnotize her,' Renee said. 'We were just trying to let her know, silently, what would happen if she opened her mouth.'

Jan was blinking back tears.

'What is she talking about?' I asked her.

'You said we'd tell. You all did. You promised.'

'Tell who what?'

'Everybody. About us not being boys. We promised Miss Vincent we'd do it after the Play-off.'

I looked away from her and hardened my heart.

'*You* promised Miss Vincent,' I said. '*We* didn't promise her a thing.'

'Tammy, that's not –'

'Who's Miss Vincent?' said Didi.

While the others took turns telling her, Renee and I looked at each other, remembering what Mr Martinelli had said.

Even after four separate versions, Didi obviously hadn't grasped the problem. 'So all you have to do is explain to Miss Vincent,' she said.

'Didi, darling,' Renee began patiently while everyone else tried to reason with Jan. I tuned out and stared mournfully into space, thinking, Steve, you're supposed to be our manager and where are you when we need you? Out on a date, that's where. Then I thought, Hold it there, Tammy, he's only the manager, you're the leader. Even Renee said so. So I thought of something. Not one of my great inspirations; just the best I could do. I stood up.

'Tygers,' I announced, 'I have hammered out a compromise. Jan, stop crying into your pizza and listen.'

I must have sounded more confident than I felt, because everyone looked up.

'What are we supposed to do when we get back home?' I asked.

'Tape "Let Me Out" and send it to New York,' said Caroline.

'Tell the other kids who we are,' said Jan.

'Right,' I said. 'Now, the kids are in Rocky Point, and the record company is in New York. So why not do both?'

'But, Tammy,' Jan said, 'I heard what Mr Martinelli said about boys selling records –'

'Did we ever promise we'd tell a record company who we are?'

'Well, no.' Jan looked confused, but suspicious.

Scott leaned forward. 'Honestly, Jan, I think she's right. After all, it's just making a record.'

'Yeah,' said Monica. 'If we can fake being boys in person, we can sure do it on a tape.'

'Listen,' I pleaded. 'We'll go home. We'll tape the song, and when Miss Vincent gives the word, we'll tell everybody in Rocky Point. We'll be Taminetta and the Tygresses or whatever you want – we'll just be Tommy and the Tygers for one little old forty-five, just so we can say we've done it.'

'Well –' Jan said, looking more surrounded than convinced, 'but what if they find out later, the record company I mean?'

'We would have told them if they asked,' Caroline said.

'I guess it might work,' grumbled Renee. 'They're not going to send someone to our school assembly when we go back home. And we did get almost to the top in the Play-off, so we'll have to play at the assembly. Then Miss Vincent will announce that we have something to tell them, and then we'll drop our little bomb. And the school will explode.'

'Not necessarily,' said Scott.

'How else do we tell them?' I asked bitterly. 'Take an ad in the paper?'

'Tell Mary Beth Hansen.'

'Scott,' I said, 'you are a genius.'

I bit into my pizza. It tasted delicious, and we had even forgotten to say no anchovies. Maybe I like anchovies after all. I just never gave them a chance.

The compromise worked – anyway, it has so far. We taped 'Let Me Out' as soon as we got back, and sent it to New York. Caroline was elected to tell Mary Beth, thus becoming the first person in history to see Mary Beth Hansen speechless – but not for long. By the time school started again, everybody knew; half the kids believed it and half of them didn't, but there was no one who hadn't heard.

At the assembly, Miss Vincent just said, 'Ladies and Gentlemen, may I introduce the Tygers,' and we each went up to the mike and said our name. There was so much laughter and clapping and cheering and booing that it took Miss Vincent five minutes to restore order, which must be some kind of a record; but it really wasn't so bad. There were lots more cheers than boos. Of course, poor Scott got teased the most, about how he was really a girl and so forth, but that's died down now; and everybody's really impressed that we made a record.

All our parents came to that assembly to hear our concert, including Renee's mother. I heard her saying to Dr Austin afterwards, 'Why, the child is almost presentable. I mean, she has *possibilities*, darling.'

The rest of our parents seemed proud, too, though they were nicer about it. In fact, we are all going to music camp this summer, except for Renee. Her father says she has to go with them to a conference in London, so she can start learning some manners. He said it, I didn't.

Anyway, we did it. We cut a record in New York during spring vacation. Making a record is a lot harder than you might think. You don't just do your number and have it taped, it's not like that at all. Jan cried three times, and I promised Scott I wouldn't tell, so I'll just say that Renee is the only one who didn't cry even once.

'Didi Darling' was released a month ago. It hasn't exactly made the charts – except around here, where we nosed Bruce Springsteen out of the number four spot last Saturday, and how do you like *that*? – but where you live, if instead of playing the top thirty on Saturday morning the DJ decided to play the top 130, then you just might hear it.

We call ourselves just the Tygers now, and we wear the same costumes, although we did have to make new vests, because some of us are still growing. We get plenty of jobs, which they will be playing without me if I can't get my geometry grade up. This Learning Module I'm in has a lot of things called New Approaches, but so far they haven't come up with a New Approach to geometry.

Wish me luck. Even a Born Leader needs that.